DEGRADATION OF THE WORLD
THE PATH TO IT AND THE PATH OUT OF IT

I See Far™

by

a Friend of Medjugorje

SPECIAL STATEMENT

Caritas of Birmingham is not acting on behalf of the Catholic Church or placing its mission under the Church. Its mission is to reach all people of the earth. Its actions are outside of the Church done privately. It is further stated:

So as not to take for granted the credibility of the Medjugorje Apparitions, it is stated that the Medjugorje apparitions are not formally approved by the Catholic Church.

Medjugorje Status
May 25, 2020 A.D.

No attempt is intended to pre-empt the Church on the validity of the Medjugorje Apparitions. They are private revelation waiting the Church's final judgment[1]. In the interim, these private revelations **are** allowed by, and for, the faithful to have devotion to and to be spread legally by the Church. Devotion and the propagation of private revelations can be forbidden only <u>if</u> the private revelation is condemned because of anything it contains which contravenes faith and morals according to AAS 58 (1966) 1186 Congregation for the Doctrine of the Faith. Medjugorje has not been condemned nor found to have anything against faith or morals, therefore it is in the grace of the Church to be followed by the faithful. By the rite of Baptism one is commissioned and given the authority to evangelize. *"By Baptism they share in the priesthood of Christ, in His prophetic and royal mission."*[2] One does not need approval to promote or to have devotions to private revelations or to spread them when in conformity to AAS 58 (1966) 1186, as the call to evangelize is given when baptized. These apparitions have not been approved formally by the Church. Caritas of Birmingham, the Community of Caritas and all associated with it, realize and accept that the final authority regarding the Queen of Peace, Medjugorje and happenings related to the apparitions, rests with the Holy See in Rome. We at Caritas, willingly submit to that judgment. While having an amiable relationship with the Diocese of Birmingham and a friendly relationship with its bishop, Caritas of Birmingham as a lay mission is not officially connected to the Diocese of Birmingham, Alabama, just as is the Knights of Columbus.[3] The Diocese of Birmingham's official position on Caritas is neutral and holds us as Catholics in good standing.

1. The Church does not have to approve the apparitions. The Church can do as She did with the apparitions of Rue du Bac in Paris and the Miraculous Medal. The Church never approved these apparitions. She gave way to the people's widespread acceptance of the Miraculous Medal and thereby the Apparitions to St. Catherine. *Sensus Fidelium* (Latin, meaning "The Sense of the Faithful"), regarding Medjugorje, is that the "sense" of the people says that "Mary is here (Medjugorje)."
2. Catechism of the Catholic Church Second Edition.
3. The Knights of Columbus also are not officially under the Church, yet they are very Catholic. The Knights of Columbus was founded as a lay organization in 1882, with the basic Catholic beliefs. Each local council appeals to the local Ordinary to be the Chaplain. The Knights of Columbus is still a lay organization, and operates with its own autonomy.

Published with permission from SJP Lic. COB.

Ninth Printing—Expanded

© 2020, S.J.P. Lic. C.O.B. © 2004, S.J.P. Lic. C.O.B.
© 2015, S.J.P. Lic. C.O.B. © 2002, S.J.P. Lic. C.O.B.
© 2013, S.J.P. Lic. C.O.B. © 1997, S.J.P. Lic. C.O.B.
© 2011, S.J.P. Lic. C.O.B.
© 2009, S.J.P. Lic. C.O.B.
© 2007, S.J.P. Lic. C.O.B.

ISBN: 978-1-878909-43-5

DTTUMAKCTJJJJABC March, 1997

Printed and bound in the United States of America.

For additional copies, contact your local bookstore or call
Caritas of Birmingham at 205-672-2000 USA.

DEGRADATION OF THE WORLD
THE PATH TO IT AND THE PATH OUT OF IT

I See Far™

by

a Friend of Medjugorje

Published with permission from SJP by
CARITAS OF BIRMINGHAM
STERRETT, ALABAMA 35147 USA

About the Witness

Many who will read these books have been following the writings of a Friend of Medjugorje for years. His original and unique insights into the important events of our day have won credence in hundreds of thousands of hearts around the world, with those affecting others, thereby, touching into the millions. His moral courage in the face of so many leaders caving in to the pressures of a politically correct world is not only refreshing, but, according to tens of thousands of written testimonies over 32 years, has helped to strengthen deeply those who desire to live the fullness of their Christian faith. His insights have repeatedly proven prophetic, having their source in the apparitions of the Virgin Mary in Medjugorje. Deeply and personally influenced by the events surrounding Medjugorje, he gave himself to the prayerful application of the words of the Virgin Mary into his life. He has spoken all over the world on Our Lady's messages and how to put them into everyday life. He came to understand that Our Lady was sent by God to speak to mankind in this time because the dangers man is facing are on a scale unlike any the world has ever known since Noah and the flood. He is not an author. He is a witness of what Our Lady has shown him to testify to—first, by his life—secondly, through the written word. He is not one looking in from the outside regarding Medjugorje, but one who is close to the events—many times, right in the middle of the events about which he has written.

Originally writing to only a few individuals in 1987, readership has grown well into the millions in the United States and in over 130 foreign countries, who follow the spiritual insights and direction given through these writings.

When asked why he signs only as "a Friend of Medjugorje," he stated:

"I have never had an ambition or desire to write. I do so only because God has shown me, through prayer, that He desires this of me. So from the beginning, when I was writing to only a few people, I prayed to God and promised I would not sign anything; that the writings would have to carry themselves and not

be built on a personality. I prayed that if it was
God's desire for these writings to be inspired and
known, then He could do it by His Will and grace
and that my will be abandoned to it.

"The Father has made these writings known and
continues to spread them to the ends of the earth.
These were Our Lord's last words before ascend-
*ing: '**Be a witness to the ends of the earth.**' These*
writings give testimony to that desire of Our Lord,
to be a witness with one's life. It is not important
to be known. It is important to do God's Will."

For those who require "ownership" of these writings by
the 'witness' in seeing his name printed on this work in
order to give it more credibility, we, Caritas of Birmingham and the Community of Caritas, state that we cannot
reconcile the fact that these writings are producing
hundreds of thousands of conversions, and will easily be
into the millions, through God's grace. His writings are
requested worldwide from every corner of the earth.
His witness and testimony, therefore, will not take credit
for a work that, by proof of the impact these writings
have to lead hearts to conversion, has been Spirit–in–

spired, with numbers increasing yearly, sweeping as a wave across the ocean. Indeed, in this case, crossing every ocean of the earth. Our Lady gave this Witness a direct message, through the Medjugorje visionary, Marija, and part of what Our Lady said to him was to **"...witness not with words but through humility..."** (Oct. 6, 1986) It is for this reason that he wishes to remain simply, "A Friend of Medjugorje."

In order to silence the voice of this witness, darkness has continually spewed out slanders to prevent souls from reading his convicting and life-changing writings. For if these writings were not so, darkness would ignore them or even lead people to them. But Jesus promised persecution to all those who follow Him, and the same will be to those who follow His Mother. *"If they persecuted me, they will also persecute you."* John 15:20

As a witness in real-time of Our Lady's time on earth, his witness and writings will continue to speak—voicing Our Lady's Way to hundreds of millions not yet born—in the centuries to come.

— Caritas of Birmingham

Acknowledgement

God alone deserves the credit for the publication of this book. It is from Him that the messages are allowed to be given through Our Lady to all of mankind. He alone deserves the praise and honor.

Special thanks and gratitude to Fred and Carol, who, through their love and generosity, provided the grant for the first edition which has perpetuated the nineth printing of this book. May God reward them one-hundredfold.

Important

To understand this book fully, please read the following:

The Blessed Virgin Mary is the Mother of Jesus. She is fondly referred to as Our Lady. The Virgin Mary or "Our Lady" began appearing daily to six children in former Yugoslavia on June 24, 1981. Our Lady informed the children that She would be giving messages to the world, as never before since the beginning of man and that these were the last apparitions on earth. The tiny village of Medjugorje began to be transformed through the visits of Our Lady. The Communists, who then ruled former Yugoslavia, to which today's Bosnia and Herzegovina also belonged, were suspicious and persecuted the visionaries. They attempted to stop what can now be considered the most important event since the early beginning of Christianity. People began to flock to the village in massive numbers. News organizations around the world began to take notice as the daily apparitions continued: *Time Magazine, Reader's Digest, Newsweek, Life Magazine, National Geographic, Wall Street Journal*, ABC, NBC, CBS, BBC London and hundreds of others reported about this site and visited it. The village of Medjugorje has now been visited by over 20 million pilgrims, and the fruit of the apparitions is proving it to be the center for **the spiritual renewal for the entire world.** In 1987, Our Lady began to give messages to the world on the 25th of each month. Through various sources, these monthly messages are spread to virtually every inhabited place on earth within hours from the moment Our Lady announces them. These messages are showing the world how to go deeper into the Christian life in a world that is sinking deeper and deeper into sin and evil.

Now 34 years* later, all of the visionaries are adults and all are married and having children.

---

* This was originally written in 1996. We only updated the year in our reprinting. Often many of these writings are foreseen, even prophetic, by realizing when it was originally written – which the update could make you think it was written in hindsight rather than foresight.

Three of the six visionaries still receive daily apparitions. The other three receive apparitions only at certain times during the year. The three who still daily see Our Lady are **Vicka, Ivan, and Marija.** The other three, who no longer see Her daily, but only on special occasions, are Ivanka, Mirjana, and Jakov. Throughout these writings, these visionaries will be quoted.

In January of 1987, Our Lady announced that She is bringing to the world a "plan for the salvation of mankind," especially during these turbulent times. She tells us that we cannot comprehend the greatness of <u>all</u> of our individual roles in this plan. Without a doubt, Medjugorje has changed, is continuing to change, and will forevermore change the world.

These writings are based on the messages given by the Virgin Mary in Medjugorje. When you read bold print with indented sentences in the paragraphs, these are Our Lady's words.

A Special Note

What you are about to read has been prayed about for years. A great deal of discernment through Our Lady's messages and the Holy Spirit has gone into its contents. In our books and newsletters, we have often recommended praying to the Holy Spirit for understanding; however, the following should not even be begun until it can be read slowly, in a contemplative way, and without interruptions. As you read it, become part of it. Find some quiet time or place such as in front of the Blessed Sacrament or some other place of solitude. If you are a Protestant, you may wish to meditate and pray to the Holy Spirit for several moments. If you are not sure of God, pray in your heart to the God you do not know. He will manifest Himself to you. Also, this book was not written to be read one time only. It is to be read several times and each time it is read, you will gain more understanding than the previous reading. It would be wise to put off reading this material until after much prayer. The Holy Spirit will provide the necessary enlightenment and strength to understand, and even to endure, the truth, which was masterfully hidden from us but is now exposed to the light by Our Lady through Her messages. Remember, the following should only be read slowly, after prayer to the Holy Spirit, and from the heart to grasp its full meaning.

Table of Contents

VI   IMPORTANT

IX   A SPECIAL NOTE

PART ONE
DEGRADATION OF THE WORLD — THE
PATH TO IT AND THE PATH OUT OF IT

CHAPTER ONE
3   A MORAL SOCIETY TO AN IMMORAL ONE,
HOW DID IT HAPPEN?

CHAPTER TWO
13   NATIONS WILL NOT LEGISLATE SOCIETY'S
ILLS AWAY. WHICH PRESIDENT IS ELECTED
NO LONGER MATTERS; RATHER ONLY
PRAYER!

PART TWO
I SEE FAR™

CHAPTER THREE
27   THE GREAT CRIME!

CHAPTER FOUR
35   THE THEFT OF MAN; THE INSTRUMENT
USED FOR THE CRIME

CHAPTER FIVE

45   CAN "THINGS" BE EVIL?

CHAPTER SIX

59   WORDS TELL MARY'S INTENTIONS WORDS
     TELL THE MEDIUM'S INTENTIONS

CHAPTER SEVEN

67   WHAT HAPPENS WHEN ALL CULTURES
     BECOME THE SAME?

CHAPTER EIGHT

79   A PRIEST DISCOVERS THE TRUTH

CHAPTER NINE

85   IF SAINTS ARE MADE SO BY THE CHURCH
     BECAUSE THEY LIVE THE SPIRIT OF TRUTH,
     ARE THEIR WORDS NOT ALSO TO BE
     ACCEPTED AS THE SPIRIT OF TRUTH?

CHAPTER TEN

99   THE TRUTH FROM THOSE IN THE INDUSTRY
     ABOUT THE MEDIUM

CHAPTER ELEVEN

107 THE UNCOVERING OF THE MEDIUM WHAT
     DOES SCIENCE REVEAL?

CHAPTER TWELVE

123 SOUNDS OF SILENCE

CHAPTER THIRTEEN

135 THE EDUCATION MYTH

CHAPTER FOURTEEN

141 OK, I ACCEPT EVERYTHING STATED, I'LL
ONLY WATCH RELIGIOUS BROADCASTING
OR TAPES

CHAPTER FIFTEEN

153 YOU'VE READ WHAT THE MESSAGES, SAINTS,
SCIENCE, AND THE SECULAR SAY ABOUT THE
MEDIUM; BUT WHAT ABOUT THE BIBLE?

CHAPTER SIXTEEN

171 IS THERE ANY DEFENSE LEFT FOR YOU
KEEPING THE TV?

CHAPTER SEVENTEEN

185 WHAT WE CAN'T DO AND CAN DO

CHAPTER EIGHTEEN

193 EXORCISM?

CHAPTER NINETEEN

203 ARE YOU USING THE MEDIUM TO BABYSIT?

CHAPTER TWENTY

221 A REVOLUTION TO BEGIN!

PART THREE

CHAPTER TWENTY-ONE
233 OUR LADY DOESN'T TEXT, SHE CALLS.
CAN YOU HEAR HER?

CHAPTER TWENTY-TWO
269 ARE YOU REALLY AGAINST CHILD ABUSE?

CHAPTER TWENTY-THREE
281 WE ARE DECEIVED

CHAPTER TWENTY-FOUR
291 THE BEST TOY A CHILD CAN HAVE IS
ANOTHER CHILD

CHAPTER TWENTY-FIVE
305 WHAT THE EXPERTS AND EXECUTIVES ARE
SAYING

CHAPTER TWENTY-SIX
323 ELECTDEMONICS
WHO DO YOU FOLLOW?

332 LINGERING QUESTIONS, COMMENTS, AND
THE ANSWERS

359 ENDNOTES

Part One

Degradation Of The World — The Path To It And The Path Out Of It

"It has become obvious how the degradation of society that took 800 years to sink the Roman Empire could sink us in one generation."

*A letter from
Davison, Michigan*

CHAPTER ONE

A Moral Society To An Immoral One, How Did It Happen?

Somehow, so deceptively, a whole generation has lost its family values, traditions, and roots. We have gone through an era where everything was questioned, changed or compromised as never before in history. The fabric of what makes up family was redefined and everyone is touched by it. What the family is defined to be today would not only have been abnormal for previous generations but also absurd.

Tragically, the family has become a democracy of individuals with no real direction except that of society. Today's society and culture dictate that the function of a family is to seek as much pleasure and worldly happiness as it wants. To be normal today is to live abnormally in contrast to untold generations before us. Even Christian families have lost the sense of what it really means to live the Christian life. Many are struggling to do so but with <u>everything</u> in society and even things in their homes, such as TV, magazines, etc., contradicting every gain, it seems that it is impossible to live our conversion. How did society end up so far from true Christian life? It's because families quit living the truth. We, as a nation (as well as the rest of the world), started to make the decision, several decades ago, that God was no longer part of our lives and should be excluded from society. Many began to assert that God and society were separate, God has nothing to do with government, etc.

How did a God-fearing nation turn away from Him so quickly and lose its spirit of righteousness? We became interested in modern attitudes. satan, so coy, so cunning, masterfully deceived us, and few are able to see what he has done. Our Lady's strongest message has been to pray. Those who have are beginning to realize more and more what is really happening. Indeed, the more we pray, the more we will grasp this book. Everyone would agree satan could not deliver a moral society to its present state without a long-range plan.

Fifty years ago,* abortion, murder, corruption, pornography and the multitude of evils plaguing our society would never have been tolerated. Society would have revolted. satan was well aware of this so he seduced us to change our attitudes and our tolerance levels. We became attracted to modern conveniences, going to ball games and the movies. Instead of going fishing with our children, we watched Andy Griffith and Opie go on TV. It was fun, wholesome, exciting and wonderful. Air conditioning took us off the front porch and brought us into the house and made it even more comfortable

* This is referring to when this book was originally written in 1994.

to sit and watch good shows like "I Love Lucy" on TV. All these things, in themselves, were not necessarily bad, but a great deception was taking place. It was calculated, planned and nurtured over time. We became busier, more engrossed in pleasure, and the television introduced us to a whole new, exciting, fascinating world... And as a fish that sees the worm, eats it, and then realizes, to its own demise, that it's hooked, we, too, have taken the bait but never even saw the hook. Why?

When we left our back yards and quit spending time with our families on our front porches and became busier and busier, we simply quit praying. Because of this, we lost the grace to see the hook. We decided to become reliant on man for our needs and less reliant on God. We were finding answers for everything — vaccines for polio, new materials like plastics, new technology for landing on the moon, new inventions to make life easier — but all the while, life was really getting harder and more complicated. Suddenly many were trying to figure out whether it was better to bring a child into the world to starve or to abort it. TV brought many questions to us, which were very simply and clearly answered a few decades before but had suddenly become so complicated. As gradually as television programming, such as "I Love Lucy" and "Andy Griffith," gave way to these things, it also gave way to showing suggestive innocence, kissing scenes, cute things — nothing really objectionable until we realize it desensitized us. After the cutesy scenes came longer sensual kissing scenes, which led to programs like "Peyton Place" and that led to the blatant evil scenes now appearing before us. satan's evil intentions were there all along while he pulled his little red wagon of false innocence.

About the same time we became engrossed in these things and quit praying as a people, we excluded God. We chose man's ideals to form society,

rather than God's ideals. God gave us what we
wanted.

In the Old Testament, the people of Israel
wanted a king to rule them, instead of the judges,
but the Prophet Samuel told the people God did
not want to give them a king. They still insisted
they wanted a king. To the displeased Samuel, the
Lord said: ***"Grant the people's every request. It is
not you they reject, they are rejecting me as their
king. As they have treated me constantly from
the day I brought them up from Egypt to this day,
deserting me and worshipping strange gods, so do
they treat you too. Now grant their request; but
at the same time, warn them solemnly and in-
form them of the rights of the king who will rule
them."*** Samuel warned the people of the harm
which would come to them and their children, but
the people refused to listen. They still wanted a
king. The Lord said***: "Grant their request and ap-
point a king to rule them."*** Later, they learned first

hand how merciless this king was and they suffered greatly because of him. They rejected God's plan to structure their nation and the result was disastrous, causing much bitterness for them.

We are no different from these Israelites. We separated God from our government, our schools, and our institutions and, by doing so, God, respecting our free will, has allowed us to choose. Now we have inherited a Godless society built by man, fractured with problems and issues that should never have been had we put God first in our lives and prayed. Officials are giving remedies which have not worked and <u>will not</u> work because they exclude God. The answer to all problems is to pray to know the Will of God and to do it. **All order, civil, spiritual, and natural, will fall into place when we, as individuals, seek God's Will.** We won't get this from television but from prayer. The quagmire the world is in now is because man wanted to do it himself. The world is in such a crisis that God has decided to

send Our Lady to pull it out from the path of suicide on which it is headed. Our Lady said:

February 17, 1984

> **"My children, pray! The world has
> been drawn into a great whirlpool. It
> does not know what it is doing. It does
> not realize in what sin it is sinking. It
> needs your prayers so that I can pull it
> out of this danger."**

"This past year I have 'fallen away' in my prayer, fasting, and devotion to living as our Father urges us through Mary. The results have been my 'falling' into a sinful lifestyle again. Much of this sinfulness is a direct result of what you wrote of in <u>I See Far</u>. As only those who have experienced such awakenings through or by the Holy Spirit can relate to, reading this book was my second 'great call' to renew my passion for a Christian way of life."

A letter from
Cincinnati, Ohio

Nations Will Not Legislate Society's Ills Away. Which President Is Elected No Longer Matters; Rather Only Prayer!

The world is certainly going in a disastrous direction which is due to man's sins.

We may think, *"Why am I to blame? I don't believe in the acceptance of abortion or illicit-life-styles."* The truth of the matter is the explosive increase of these sins is the fault of all of us. Through us, these great sins have manifested themselves blatantly! When we quit praying, we became less holy. We may never have been really bad, but we gradually became a less holy people in the Fifties, Sixties and Seventies. Because of the lack of the virtue of holiness, we became more prone to sin even though many of us continued to go to church and most of us considered ourselves okay. Yet, it was not through our committing great sins, but through our lack of holiness, that we, as Christians, allowed the breeding ground for the great sins of our society. The illicit life-styles, who blatantly expose themselves in parades, could never do this in an environment of holiness. Unholiness supports them. Our Lady calls us to be light and has said:

March 14, 1985

> **"...I am calling you to the light, which you should carry to all the people who are in darkness. People who are in darkness daily come into your homes. Dear children, give them the light!..."**

Unfortunately our environment is permeated with darkness, but darkness cannot dwell in the presence of light.

Virtually everyone has been influenced by someone in their life who has made an impression on them. In the presence of someone who is holy, we are on our best behavior. Their light, their holiness, inspires us toward this. Their witness is powerful enough to cause change and suppress darkness. What swearer cursed in the presence of Mother Teresa?

<u>No</u> politician, <u>no</u> government is going to remedy any of our present problems. **WE ARE,** through Our Lady and Her messages. The world spends billions for programs to remedy our problems — drugs, crime, teenage pregnancy, AIDS, etc. Politicians offer answers, which would fill up the world's libraries, and yet we have the answer to <u>all</u> these problems. It is very simple. The answer to drugs is holiness; to teenage pregnancy, holiness; to AIDS, holiness. The answer is very simple, and we must uncomplicate things and just be holy. Our Lady said:

December 25, 1989

> **"...For years I have been calling you to
> encourage you to a profound spiritual
> life in simplicity,..."**

Through our living a life of holiness, Our
Lady commissions us to bring something wonderful
to the whole world, something for which the whole
world yearns, something for which the very heart
of man is craving. We are to rejoice because it will
come from God, through us, for the world. Our
Lady said:

June 24, 1992

> **"...You are the ones who will bring
> peace to the world."**

We have toyed with so many new things and
accepted them, never having the foresight that they
would lead to the destruction of the family and
society. Not having this wisdom was the fruit of

not praying. We didn't pray because we were more fascinated with the TV, etc. Our Lady said:

July 30, 1987

>**"...Children, darkness reigns over the whole world. People are attracted by many things and they forget about the more important..."**

The human race is in grave danger, headed for disastrous ruin. Our Lady goes to the extreme and says there is only one way to save it from its present direction. She said:

July 30, 1987

>**"...Prayer is the only way to save the human race."**

The world is in a tangle, and it cannot get free on its own. It is being strangled by its own doing. However, God, in His mercy, will help us. This can be compared to a little boy playing with his mother's ball of yarn. First, he slowly toys with it but gets more and more tangled in it. While struggling to get free from it, he becomes more tangled and endangers himself with strangulation. Hearing him choking, his mother runs to his rescue but cannot free him immediately because of the risk of choking him further and doing permanent harm. So she works with all the speed, patience, intensity and concern she can, delicately untangling this string and severing another, detaching the strings one by one, with a steady hand, until she gets to the string around his neck and frees him. The child saw absolutely no danger in the ball of yarn and, in fact, couldn't have seen the potential danger.

Just as the mother came to her child's rescue, Mary is sent to the world which is choking with sin. The family is so entangled that to make any rapid moves would run the risk of breaking up the family and causing more harm. So with intensity, concern, patience, and speed, Our Lady delicately begins freeing us from the stranglehold of the society man has built, knowing all the while if the process moves too quickly it will rupture relationships. In Her wisdom, She initiates our formation through prayer and, in this way, She slowly frees us. There are casualties along the way because of obstinate hearts who refuse the grace to change and make a clean break with the direction in which the world is going, yet others go forward. It is a tragedy for those who stay behind and "die" (rejecting Our Lady's plan) during the process, just as it would be for the patient who dies on the operating table. It is the reason Our Lady said Jesus offers us a way which is bitter; but through this bitterness we will discover sweetness by getting rid of the petty things in our lives which will open our hearts to be changed.

July 25, 1987

> **"...Dear children, pray and accept**
> **all that God is offering you on a way**
> **which is bitter. But at the same time,**

God will reveal every sweetness to whomever begins to go on that way, and He will gladly answer every call of God. Do not attribute importance to petty things..."

Yet, when a family commits to Our Lady, the way will be sweet and joyful. Our Lady said:

August 5, 1985:

"...Give your utmost and we will go together, sensitive to the sweetness of life, light, and joy..."

What must we do to change our direction? First of all, reject those things which led us onto this path.

The Bible speaks of a time in the end when there will be a great increase of knowledge in man, but they will know nothing. It is difficult to see how anyone who is in a spirit of prayer cannot see that we are in such times, with schools and universities corrupting the minds of the youth. We can begin to understand why St. Francis refused to allow his people to be educated by institutions of his day. We must show the same concern St. Francis showed. The test we must pass is that of Holiness. It is the reason we are put here on the Earth. <u>All</u> else is <u>trivial</u> and means nothing in the end. satan wants to drive us far from Christian life and will do everything to make us think our job, our home, our financial security is important. In reality, these things mean nothing...absolutely nothing, because passing the test of Holiness, during this brief moment of life, will prove at our graduation of this life into the next to be the only test which mattered. All else of the world is fruitless...

September 25, 1992

"...In a 'special way,' he (satan) wishes to destroy your souls. He wishes to guide you as far away as possible from

Christian life as well as from the commandments, to which the Church is calling you, so you may live them. satan wishes to destroy everything which is holy in you and around you. Therefore, little children, pray, pray, pray..."

We cannot just empty ourselves and not refill. It is a mistake to think, *"Okay, I'll quit doing everything unholy."* This is only half the process. We must replace these things with holy acts and deeds and live holiness by our very lives, because our families, friends, nation, and the world will depend on our witness for eternity.

Part Two

I See Far™

"After reading <u>I See Far</u>, everything is clear.
I have for years had the feeling or knowledge
that the world is way out of control and way
off balance when it comes to God and liv-
ing according to His ways. There is such a
monstrous difference between the way I was
taught and the way the people of today think.
I often wonder what happened to the people
who were brought up as I was. Where are
they? Doesn't anyone think about God and
the Commandments as Sacred and Holy any-
more? I have often thought that it can't go on
this way much longer. God is going to have to
do something."

A letter from
Hilbert, Wisconsin

CHAPTER THREE

The Great Crime!

Seeing where this book leads may be almost unbearable; therefore, some may wish to deny the following. Nevertheless, with Our Lady and following the steps of Her messages and the logic contained within them, inflamed by the Holy Spirit, the truth will come forth in any heart who seeks it. Upon completing this, it will be much easier to understand why Our Lady said:

April 4, 1985

> **"...I wish to keep on giving you messages as it has never been in history from the beginning of the world..."**

Coming upon the crime scene, the detective knew nothing. As he began the work of investigating, it soon became evident he was dealing with a premeditated crime and the perpetrator and motive behind it were masterfully concealed. With all crimes, evidence exists and soon, with hard work, small, infinitesimal pieces of information began to add up. Alone, these shreds of evidence meant nothing — a footstep in the dirt, a piece of clothing, etc. — but added together, they began to reveal more and more truth. Each item, like a piece of a puzzle, showed nothing, but once put together, the full picture could be seen. With all the evidence collected, it was easy for the detective to see the truth and know who was guilty.

Something has happened in the world today which has been masterfully concealed. A crime of such magnitude that many pieces of the puzzle, from so many different sources, must be brought together to even begin to see the picture. However, once collected, assembled, and combined with an open heart, the jolting truth becomes clear that we on earth have been so masterfully deceived.

In the Book of Job, we read how satan appeared before the throne of God and conversed with God. He made a request to God, Who granted his request to test His holy Job for a time. satan tried to make Job turn from God by putting him through many tests.

One day Pope Leo XIII, after celebrating Holy Mass, was in conference with some cardinals, and he suddenly sank to the floor. A physician, who was nearby, thought he was dead as he felt no pulse. However, he did come to and, with great emotion, he said: *"Oh, what a horrible picture I have been permitted to see."* [1] What Pope Leo saw was satan talking to God, and he heard the voice of satan asking God for a time with the Church, just as satan did in the Scriptures with Job. Pope Leo heard satan ask for a century in order to turn the Church

from God, and his request was granted. The Pontiff
had this vision toward the end of the 19th century,
and it cannot be discounted that satan and God
may have had this conversation centuries or even a
thousand years before. No one can be certain; however, it was stated to Pope Leo that the 19th and 20th
century is satan's and spanning back 60 centuries,
it would be extremely difficult to defend that it has
not belonged to him. When one considers Scripture — that satan requested Job and God granted
it — could we possibly not believe it also for God to
grant a century to satan?

The visionary, Mirjana, related that satan
appeared to her and tried to tempt her to **renounce**
Our Lady. When Mirjana rejected him, Our Lady
immediately appeared to her and said:

Before December 26, 1982

> **"Excuse me for this, but you must
> realize that satan exists. One day he**

appeared before the throne of God and asked permission to submit the Church to a period of trial. God gave him permission to try the Church for one century. This century is under the power of the devil, but when the secrets confided to you come to pass, his power will be destroyed. Even now he is beginning to lose his power and has become aggressive. He is destroying marriages, creating division among priests and is responsible for obsessions and murder. You must protect yourselves against these things through fasting and prayer, especially community prayer. Carry blessed objects with you. Put them in your house, and restore the use of holy water."

With our limited intelligence, we want as much time as possible to prepare for any major task or feat we wish to accomplish. It is with simple logic that a far superior intellect would have enough sense to conclude the same. Perhaps for a long time, satan planned and schemed all his deceptions, as carefully as a criminal, to cover his tracks and to hide all evidence to capture man, who was totally unaware. Small pieces of evidence show up, even in the late 1800s, of his preparations and plans to dominate and control the events of this century. Perhaps Our Lady is appearing in the latter part of this century in preparation for the next century, to take what satan has amassed and destroy it, as we go into the next century, during which She will reign and dominate.

"I have been reading I See Far. It was very hard to accept at first, but the more I read the more I began to see that many of these thoughts have run through my mind long before I read this. I pushed them aside, thinking I was getting a little bit odd in my old age, but now I see God has been speaking to me all along, trying to get my attention. I See Far gave me just that — the ability to see far. Everyone must read this. It will be a priority for me to help everyone in my family see now what I see. Thanks!"

A letter from
Orlando, Florida

CHAPTER FOUR

The Theft Of Man; The Instrument Used For The Crime

If we accept what Pope Leo heard, what the visionaries of Medjugorje say, and many other things as proof that satan had been given power in the world as never before, it is reasonable that he would follow simple concepts. The Pied Piper story contains all the elements he needs to entice and mesmerize people into following him. Just as the Pied Piper allured, entranced and entertained the rats into following him right into the water to their death by drowning, so, too, is satan's desire to cleverly lead people, without a hint of their impending danger, to spiritual death. What would be necessary? The Pied Piper had his pipe. satan would have to come up with his creation. He would also have to have a trap, a net, which would take a lot of work to ensnare all the people together; but once captured, they could be **"net-worked"** together to listen to his pipe so he could lead them. One rotten apple in a bushel basket will spoil those next to it, and those, in turn, would further infect those surrounding them. Space between the apples would slow or stop this process. This master intellect understood clearly that without a network tying all people together, his plan to infect every man possible would become too difficult. So the concept of networking and the ideals in the Pied Piper story were the foundation upon which everything would be formed. Would not the father of witchcraft desire a **medium** through which to speak? Webster defines "medium:"

> **Medium:** a go between, intermediary, an individual held to be a channel of communication between the earthly world and a world of spirits.[2]

This medium, in order to deceive man and be able to lead him astray, would offer good, pleasurable enlightenment and, in so doing, seduce him to ruin later, after having led him astray. But would these things of his century be ideals, spiritual concepts or actual physical things of his creation?

Fortunately for us, but not the case with the rats, man is blessed with Our Lady's appearances, just as satan is leading us into the water to drown. She, through Her messages, began to tell us that we have been deceived. *"No,"* we responded, *"the music is beautiful and we're being entertained."* Our Lady relayed, through Her messages, that we've been entranced. *"No,"* we responded, *"the things the piper offers us are good."* Our Lady said there are evil things, and She began to explain gently and slowly. Many who responded to Our Lady and Her messages realized we had been masterfully duped, as were the rats. What has Our Lady been saying? What has She been exposing?

It is important to realize that the people of
former Yugoslavia, to which Bosnia and Herzegovina with Medjugorje also belonged, lived under the
terrorism and oppression of Communism. The evils
of Communism, so close at hand, would be one of
the many things we might expect Our Lady to have
mentioned but She never did. Abortion, listed as
the number-one evil in the world on many people's
list, has never been mentioned by Our Lady in a
public message. Understanding this, those remaining things, which Our Lady does mention, must be
considered with great importance. When we exam-
ine Our Lady's messages, it is extremely rare that
She mentions a **physical thing,** and it is even more
rare that She mention this "thing" more than once.
However, one thing Our Lady mentioned on several occasions, and even in a message to the world,
is some "thing" we live with daily, ignoring its bad
qualities because of its "perceived" good qualities.
It is so rooted into the fabric of our lives that its in-

fluence is no longer seen as a danger to our spiritual lives for eternity. There is only one physical **"thing"** which Our Lady tells us to **AVOID** in over fifteen years of apparitions.* She uses the word "avoid" and She Herself specifically ties this word directly and unmistakably to a material object. She said:

June 16, 1983

"Avoid television."

Once more, this was given as a rule for the purpose of growing in the spiritual life. Television is the single "thing" which Our Lady has specifically mentioned and spoken about several times. She went as far as telling us it is of **no value** and to **renounce** it. Our Lady wants us to restart and change from this moment. She "plainly" states "clearly" so that no one can misunderstand: **"Turn off the television"** and let Lent be the incentive to do this be-

---

* This was originally written in 1994. A Friend of Medjugorje's writings often relate to the future, even prophetically, which becomes apparent in the present when one realizes the date it was originally written.
— The Community of Caritas

cause this weekly message for the world was given in the beginning of Lent. She does not mean to do it only for Lent. Lent is only the incentive. When we change, we must not go back to our old ways or we can never say we've changed.

February 13, 1986

> **"Dear children, this Lent is a special incentive for you to <u>change</u>. <u>Start</u> from this moment. <u>Turn off</u> the television and <u>renounce</u> various things of no value…"**

"Change," "start," "turn off," "renounce." It is of great significance that Our Lady has never mentioned the great sins and atrocities of our time, and yet boldly and strongly says to **"renounce things"** of **no value** and names **"television"** as the first example. It is first among the **"things"** to renounce. One may think, *I do not care much for TV but occasionally I may watch it.* Our Lady is telling

us something about which we may not have been
fully conscious: She wants it out of our lives. The
definition of renounce:

> **Renounce:** to give up by formal declaration,
> to refuse to follow, obey, or recognize any
> further.[3]

Our Lady could not in any way have meant only
during Lent because it is a contradiction to come
back to what you have renounced, as it is defined
in the dictionary. And if this is true in regard to
secular life, then what does renounce mean in
the spiritual life? She said to start from this moment to change. Change and do what? The word
"renounce" carries great importance; its meaning is clear, with no gray line of compromise, that
maybe Our Lady only means for us to partially
turn away. The word is too strong to minimize it to
mean something less than what it says. satan certainly knows the word "renounce," for he himself
appeared to Mirjana in order for her to renounce

Our Lady (as you've already read on page 30). So
it is now Our Lady appears in an opposite way and
tells us to renounce the television. Our Lady as-
sociates "renounce" to television through several of
Her messages but also uses the word to apply it to
that which the TV leads: bad thoughts and desires,
materialism, etc. Our Lady says:

February 22, 1988

"...Renounce sin..."

Can it be by chance that She has used the
word "renounce" for both **sin** and for **television**?
Is that in itself a message? A survey reported [4]
that when people were asked how much money it
would take for them to give up television for life,
many reported great sums and 20% said for no
amount would they renounce it. This attachment to
a "thing" tells of something in man that is fundamentally wrong. Our Lady tells us to renounce that
thing which we like the most.

December 15, 1989

"...Renounce some 'thing' that you like most."

There is something much more behind television which causes it to be the one "thing" of the world Our Lady specifically recommends and invites us to renounce.

"Our Lady of Medjugorje called for a year of the youth a few years ago. Later the Pope called for a year of the youth. Later, Our Lady called for a year of the family. Later, yet again, the Pope called for the year of the family. Next Our Lady called to renounce television, beginning in Lent of 1986. A few weeks after the tenth anniversary of Our Lady's message, Pope John Paul II, at the beginning of Lent called for a fast from TV. Many were shocked. Italian TV, with networks around the world, broadcasted his statement from his balcony. He said, along with his request:

> *'In families, the television seems to substitute rather than facilitate dialogue among people.'*

"It seems the Pope's thinking merges with the Virgin Mary's, by the power of the Holy Spirit!"

Associated Press, Monday, March 11, 1996, an eyewitness account in Italy

44

CHAPTER FIVE

Can "Things" Be Evil?

One father, who began to see what Our Lady was saying, had given a great deal of thought about TV for many months: the damage, the perceived good, etc. One day in prayer he concluded that he and his children would destroy it. He reasoned it out for an hour, while in prayer, and committed to renounce it officially and destroy it. In the last minute of the hour of prayer, having already decided what and even how to do it, the practical thought sprang upon him: *"Wait a minute. The TV is just a box. It's a thing. Things are not evil. I just can't be a kook and think this way. Perhaps I am reacting in extremism."* He put the thought aside, knowing to act in extremism was wrong, except in his love for God. Two days later, he awaited, as he does each month, for Our Lady's message on the 25th of the month to be announced. When it was, he was amazed how almost directly She confirmed his discernment.

August 25, 1992

> **"...I call upon you to open yourselves completely to me, so that through each of you I may be enabled to convert and save the world, where there is much sin and <u>many 'things'</u> which are <u>evil</u>...."**

He immediately realized that the "practical" thoughts which sprang upon him were not of God, and that it was the Holy Spirit who had prompted his first contemplation. Two days later, Our Lady's message confirmed with clear words that, yes, there are **things** which are evil. From this, he determined to carry out formally and officially his renouncement and did so afterwards.

Many times Our Lady has referred to the word, "things" in Her messages. While this includes many items, it is to Her messages we must go to see what material things of the world She has mentioned. The **TV** is the example; it holds the first place, being named directly among the things about which She has spoken. When you read Our Lady's message, you'll see the word, "thing," can first be applied to television. Even though Our Lady mentions television on several occasions, She sometimes uses simply the word "thing." The word, "television," and the word, "thing," swap out in almost all cases. It is obvious it holds the first place among the things about which She is referring. Through Her messages, you'll see how our attachment to this is so strong that it kills the spiritual life. When speaking of this, Our Lady again uses the words, "renounce" and "things" (television). She said:

February 25, 1990:

> **"...I especially want you to <u>renounce</u>**
> **all the things to which you are at-**
> **tached but are hurting your spiritual**
> **life. Therefore, little children, decide**
> **completely for God, and do not allow**
> **satan to come into your life through**
> **those things that hurt both you and**
> **your spiritual life..."**

Our Lady asks us to renounce all the things
to which we are attached and are hurting us and our
spiritual lives. Ask yourself, *"What is the foremost
thing which can do this?"* It is a dominating and
guiding force over the whole world's population. Our
Lady does not want us to obey a voice from the opposite direction any longer but to listen to Her voice.

June 16, 1983

> **"...Have them not listen to him**
> (satan)**, nor obey him. It is to the voice**

of the Blessed Virgin that they should
pay attention...."

Our Lady is coming with Her voice, and Her
message is in direct opposition to satan's voice and
his message. Our Lady wants to help us and make
us aware of satan's deception and uncover that
voice which he has put right in our midst. Our Lady
wants the truth known about this "thing," which is
being used to prevail over and in our hearts:

September 25, 1986

> **"...I am calling you, so that by your**
> **prayer and your life you help to de-**
> **stroy everything that's evil in people**
> **and <u>uncover</u> "the deception" that**
> **satan makes use of. You pray that the**
> **truth prevails in all hearts...."**

Uncover what? satan makes use of what? We
know what sin is: murder, adultery, theft, gossip,
slander, jealousy, etc. Why does Our Lady end the

above message with, *"that the truth prevails in all hearts?" What is it that we don't "see?"* Perhaps because we are so preoccupied with "this thing," She knows when we are turned to the TV, we cannot be turned to the Holy Spirit, and He cannot work in us.

May 9, 1985

> **"...Your hearts are turned toward the <u>things</u> of earth and they preoccupy you. Turn your hearts toward prayer and seek the Holy Spirit to be poured out on you..."**

However, we respond, *"I pray and can do that after I watch some programs."* Our Lady makes no bones about this. In the very beginning months of Her apparitions, She says you cannot do both.

December 8, 1981

> **"...It would be a good thing to give up television, because after seeing some**

(one or several) **programs, you are distracted and unable to pray..."**

Many may respond, *"This is too hard. Why can't we
see a little? Perhaps we can at least see the news and
read the newspaper. After all, one must be informed."*
Our Lady says:

April 17, 1986

> **"If you look at the programs, if you
> look at the newspapers, your heads are
> filled with news, then there is no longer
> any place for me in your hearts..."**

It is easy to reject the above message and dis-
count that Our Lady doesn't really mean that liter-
ally, yet, this message was given to the prayer **group,
and they, themselves, questioned Our Lady's advice**
regarding watching television and reading newspapers as too difficult. She responded with the above
words when they complained, after having already
told them not to watch TV. But still, the question

lingers. We want to be informed! Fr. Frank Poncelet, in his book, Air Waves From Hell, writes four
rationalizations people use to justify why they must
watch TV. His third rationalism addresses those
who feel they must be informed. He writes:

> **Statement:** Third Rationalization: TV is a
> necessary tool for information so that people
> can be in touch with the world...

> **Answer:** With the world, right? That is the
> whole question. TV sells you the world like
> the devil did when he tempted Christ. TV is
> intrinsically worldly, materialistic, and hu-
> manistic. It can only say, "the world is the
> world is the world. That's all there is and
> that's good enough." It trains us not to see
> God's hand, yet, while man should be in-
> formed about the society in which he lives,
> true; but what you see on TV, however, is
> not the truth. It is altered, manipulated, and
> that's not how you should inform yourself.[5]

An executive producer from one of the three major networks relayed: *"We produce shows, news documentaries, to let the viewer 'feel' they've been treated fairly and objectively, and then we can lead them in to what we want them to believe in the end."* [6]

While presently there are just a few people who recognize these things, through Our Lady's messages, there is a growing knowledge among Her children that something is fundamentally wrong regarding the television, and these few are beginning to do something about it. October, 1990, the Balthasar House was opened in Rome, Italy, to prepare young men for a life of evangelical consecration. Pope John Paul II was presented their charter by Cardinal Ratzinger. Their charter, the contract each member must sign, includes, *"There will be no television set in the house."* It adds, *"we joyfully give up much that the world considers normal and make rare use of other forms of the mass media."* [7] But what if one avoids evil programs and commer-

cials and watches only good shows and commercials then, ask yourself, for what reason does the
Balthasar House expel it altogether?

Finally this chapter raises the issue of the
theological aspect: that God made all of creation,
therefore, all is good. Some have mistranslated the
August 25, 1992 message in different languages to
sanitize it, to be "theologically in tune." However,
Our Lady's messages must be understood in light
of all Her messages. She well knows all creation is
of God, and therefore, the things from the Creator
cannot be evil. A gun can be used for good or evil
— hunting to provide for one's self or robbery to
provide one's greed. This, therefore, cannot be said
this "thing" (gun) is evil. The laws of physic, in the
way it operates and the elements it is made from is
of God's creation, therefore, not evil. However, the
equation is now before modern man of the deriva-
tive he (man) has made from God's creation — that
are things which are evil.

What is the purpose of the most common
birth control device? Lay these items on a table.
For the Christian, who understands, it is an evil
thing. Yes, it is made from God's elements found
in creation, but which were never intended for such
violations of God's natural law. The Atomic Bomb
cannot be claimed as evil. It saved many lives, even
Japanese, when they had vowed to fight to the last
man. But what of the R-42 Abortion pill? It is an
evil thing, with only one purpose. Yes, the Atomic
Bomb kills and the R-42 pill kills, but one still cannot be classed as an evil thing, while the other can
be classed as intricately evil and a disturbance of
God's creation, birthed by man's creation. It is difficult to find anything that could be described as an
evil thing before the eve of modern technology, but
now the world is beginning to accumulate things
which have no value except as evil. Human cloning
and the genetic reordering of man are only a few,
among many, of the intrinsically evil things man has

created through derivatives of God's creation. His
is holy, man's is evil (technology and development
against natural law).

Lastly, what about the tree of good and evil
that God made in the Garden of Eden? It cannot
be said it was intricately evil, for its purpose was for
man to show his love for God, through it, by obedience of not eating of it. Things today which are
evil, at the very least, should be dealt with, at least
as the same. Much more so that they are creations
of man's unbridled search to become masters of his
own destiny. The result is disaster after disaster of
society and its deterioration. There are things in
our modern world which are evil, for they have no
purpose to exist other than to exist to violate God's
natural law.

"It has been a wonderful year of change in our family as we read and live the words Our Lady has been sending us. The improvements in our lives have been tremendous as the television has been turned off and the caring for one another has become the most important aspect of our lives. We now see more clearly with adult vision the invasion that television has brought into our home and the disruption of family living. We are thankful for the insight and harmony provided by your book."

A letter from
South Bend, Indiana

CHAPTER SIX

Words Tell Mary's Intentions Words Tell The Medium's Intentions

Our Lady didn't say to partially give up television. What She wants from us is something much stronger than going part way. Our Lady says, **"avoid."** Avoid means: **expel; to depart or withdraw from; leave; to keep away from.**[8]

June 16, 1983

> **"Renounce all passions and all inordinate desires. Avoid television, particularly evil programs..."**

Again, renounce shows up in the same message with television and now, knowing the full meaning of **"avoid,"** it seems that this would be a word you

would use for an exorcism — Expel? Withdraw
from? Leave? If this century belongs to satan, is
it possible his influence so dominates all the earth,
even Christians, that Her call is for something like
an exorcism? Is the television the instrument created to lead man like the Pied Piper did with his
pipe? It is strange that after years of Our Lady's
being with us, and after years during which many
are praying and trying to do what She asks, that as
recently as July 25, 1993, we receive a message in
which She says:

July 25, 1993

> **"...I do not want satan to deceive you,**
> **for he wants to lead you the wrong**
> **way..."**

We are Her children. We don't want satan
to deceive or lead us astray either. If we are going
to Holy Mass and saying our prayers, what is Our
Lady talking about — that satan wants to lead us

astray? What is the television? What does it do to us? What possible harm can come from watching good shows? It is important to go back to the very first hour of this century, the first hour of satan's time, which we might call it if this century belongs to satan. What is recorded about that hour? What would that hour be called? That first hour which birthed a new dawn for a new century? Irving Settel in his book, A Pictorial History of Television, writes:

> *"In New York at the **witching hour** of midnight, December 31, 1899, horns blew and champagne flowed in a celebration seldom **matched for frantic joy.** This was no ordinary New Year's Eve along Broadway from Union Square to 42nd Street. Silk-hatted men, **bejeweled** women at Del Monico's, Sherry's, and Hammerstein's Paradise Roof Garden danced and drank to a new century. The change of the Number from 18 to 19 struck*

the spark. To America, the Twentieth Century
meant hope, progress, a fabulous future for
*a **lusty** nation. Everything **modern** acquired*
*the label, **'20th Century.'** Everything prior*
to 1900 became suddenly 'Victorian.' If you
were not '20th Century' in dress, deportment,
*and **daring,** you were old hat."* [9]

Witching hour, bejeweled women, frantic joy, dancing, drinking, lusty, modern, and daring would be a good description of someone who believed satan had just been given the century; however, the source quoted is purely secular. He was completely unaware of the points he showed and the cause of celebration by breaking away from the past 60 centuries to the freedom of the new world of the 20th Century. It was the rush to bring an instrument into the world to pipe a tune which causes breakthrough after breakthrough to happen.

Researching the birth of television through secular sources, one will find repeatedly the words, "miracle" and "miraculous," used. One source writes that when the human voice was carried over wire, that it was an *"invented authentic miracle."*[10] The dawn of this century is described as *a "period of swift technological advances."* [11] What suddenly catapulted men and technology? Scanning secular sources, you'll find descriptions of miraculous, accidental breakthroughs, things invented but not with the real understanding of how they worked, so the word magical was used often to describe their function such as in the following:

"It is purely electronic magic, something strange in the world and to thoughtful people rather frightening." [12]

Again, a secular source even describes television as "strange in the world," and even frightening, not to ignorant people but to thoughtful people. Could this truly be an instrument with the express purpose to captivate man, so much so that thoughtful men had the discernment that something was

disturbing about it? More evidence and pieces of
the picture are found when we look at the words
which are used for TV. They contain several elements of witchcraft and are main clues to show that
perhaps Our Lady is upon the earth to uncover
a deception. <u>The Pictorial History of Television</u>
describes television *as "modern wizardry."* [13] It is
referred to in all sources, both secular and religious,
as a **medium/media.** The meaning of **"medium"** has
already been explained as a go-between, an **intermediary,** connecting the world of earth to the world
of spirit. A spiritualist is a medium for channeling
different spirits and this can be achieved through
different **channels.** These words, when viewed as
shown, cast the "medium" as the "anti" of Our
Lady, spiritually coming to speak Her words to us.

"Today my eyes, mind, and heart have been opened as never before — I just finished reading your book I See Far. Each newsletter or book you send is wonderful — but this one was so special regarding the TV. I have turned it off and it will not be turned on again. I can't believe how so many of us were 'taken in' — myself most of all."

A letter from
North Haven, Connecticut

CHAPTER SEVEN

What Happens When All
Cultures Become The Same?

A plan of massing everyone together to infect all is also achieved through the capturing of all minds underneath this medium, TV, network. Just as fish are caught in a net, you can see when flying over communities in a small plane, all homes are tied together by air waves or cables. Regardless of culture, tradition, or heritage, all homes and institutions are tied together with those of other towns, cities, states and countries throughout the whole world. This network is the great achievement, and parallels the one, small, insignificant, rotten apple which can spread its rot throughout a whole basket of fruit. How is it that so many of the youth and adults of the world, with their radically different cultural backgrounds, are all falling into the same patterns, the same fad: family breakdowns, divorce, murder, suicide, depression, and immorality? In contrast, on an island where TV is barred, a study showed the youth of the island to be the most complete, joyful, happy, balanced youth anywhere in the world.[14] Then how is it that people of the earth with diverse backgrounds are plagued with the same patterns of problems already mentioned; and where TV is barred, the people, especially the youth, are radically different? It seems the TV itself is the means for its own message, even dictating its own lifestyles and patterns for man to imitate.

Searching the evidence several decades back, the thought from many sources was that what the TV gives is "a message." Recently, however, most all secular sources refer to it as *the medium 'is' the message."*[15] The author of the introduction of <u>Pictorial History of Television</u> states:

"It has taken a super-sophisticated triumph of man's insatiable curiosity and ingenuity to restore the message of mankind to its most primitive form." [16]

While he may be speaking of communication, man's most primitive form was based in idolatry, and TV is stated in the quote as the means to achieve it. It is not someone who is a religious who states this, rather a former CBS executive who is pro-TV. What would be behind a move of restoration (or resurrection) to bring man back to his primitive form? What is behind it obviously has its own message, and it counters Our Lady who has Her message. Which do we choose, satan and his deceptive strength, or Our Lady and Her love for us? Because of that love, shouldn't we believe Her and Her words? Our Lady tells us to decide.

November 25, 1987

"...Pray that satan does not entice you with his pride and deceptive strength. I am with you and I want you to believe me that I love you..."

The television produces prodigies that are wonders. It can show incredible things and imagery, such as earthquakes, the dead rising, and even fire coming down from the heavens. Yes, it is deceptive and not real but many are deceived and even lose a sense of reality. One small five-year-old took his father's gun, went into the kitchen, and killed his mother. [17] He did not understand why she did not get back up after seeing the TV stars get shot and reappear on the next week's series. One might think only children are deceived but these writings will show that adults are included as well.

One other word of importance to trace, in order to understand television, is the word itself. The iconoscope, invented in the beginning of this century, was called the eye because of exactly what it did. It duplicated the human eye for the TV camera, an outstanding breakthrough. So many of the inventions for TV mechanically parallel human functions. Therefore, it is easy to trace and see that these things, which have no life, duplicate that which is life, and when made up into instruments can be of great danger to man.

This was the case with Eve. She did not realize the danger because her eyes were deceived, because of desire and disobedience. The television is often referred to, in some sources, as an eye. But it is our own eyes we lend to it to be seduced. It was through the eye that the serpent brought down man the first time, and now a second time, he pulls the whole world in his grip through the eye. The first time the serpent tells Eve:

Genesis 3:5–6

> *"No, God knows well that the mo-*
> *ment you eat of it your __eyes__ will be*
> *opened.... The woman __saw__ that the*
> *tree was good for food and pleasing*
> *to the __eye__ and desirable for gaining*
> *wisdom."*

All this perfectly describes television — entertaining food for the mind, pleasing and desirable to
the eye, and, all the while, supposedly enlightening
us with wisdom — all through the eye. After both
Adam and Eve ate of the fruit, the Scripture says:

> *"Then the eyes of both of them were*
> *opened."*

They could suddenly see what they could never see
before. They could "see far" into things, when before they were kept innocently pure and protected
by the Father. They saw nakedness for the first
time. Before that, they were naked, but sensuality

did not exist. There was no perversion of the body. The "apple" changed that, just as television now is increasing and spreading the same.

Is the purpose of television the same? Is the serpent, most cunning of all creatures, not duplicating man's fall through the eye during the 19th and 20th century, as he did to Adam and Eve hundreds of centuries before? The word, "television," itself gives more evidence to help us make up our minds. Two languages which may be said to have been used for holy use were Greek and Latin. Many translations from the Bible came from the Greek language. Latin, of course, was the language of the Church for ages. Possessed people who know nothing of the language often spew out perfect vocabulary in Latin. satan always uses that which is God's in his action of opposing God. It is not proper to mix two root words from different languages, yet, the word, television, does just that. No one is quite sure what force brought about a word which offends scholars and linguists. However, its meaning may help you discern what is perhaps not traceable on a human level. The meaning is the same thing told to Eve.

> *Tele/vision: the Greek root,* **"tele,"** *means* **far.** *The Latin root,* **"video,"** *means* **"I see."** <u>*Far I see*</u>*, or once properly formed to its clear meaning, "I see far."* [18]

The serpent's promise was "your eyes will be opened," (far you'll see). Indeed, in the last and now this century, our eyes have been opened, our innocence and even that of our children is gone, because now "we see far" by the television. Perhaps in a different degree, but the same thing was offered to Eve. Is it a vision? An evil vision of the last and this century? The voice Eve heard? And to crush it, does God now send Our Lady? Is this why Our Lady specifically mentions this medium and refers to it — something She has not done except only rarely concerning material things specifically?

Most words when changed into other languages are very different. For instance, the word "can opener" can differ greatly from language to language. Strangely though, the word, television, is universally spelled and pronounced almost the same way in every language. Is it by chance that this word is the same in every language? Collect the following words in prayer: **magical, electronic wizardry, prodigies, medium/media, TV channel(ing), network, message, the eye, television.** Is this making too much over too little? Perhaps one could say that looking only at this aspect; however, all the pieces must be put together, and indictments made by the evidence itself, considering these words along with other evidence. Small pieces of evidence are in themselves minimal and mean little, until all wedded together and the full picture is seen. The deception taking place does just that, "deceives." The perpetrator destroys whatever evidence he can and keeps the rest of the evidence hidden or fragmented so there is no notice of what really took place or is taking place. Some crimes take place in view of many, others only under cover or darkness. Could it be that this is perpetrated in view of everyone, in the light, undetected?

"I do agree with you that we should avoid looking at television for it destroys some of our community life. We have no evening recreation any more since three years. My reaction was to stop looking at television. Some of the other sisters do also, but not all of them."

A letter from a nun
in Angers, France

CHAPTER EIGHT

A Priest Discovers The Truth

The Church fathers tell us, *"The eyes are the windows of the soul."* If protected, innocence dwells; and if exposed to the world, filth dwells.

Fr. Al Winshman, S.J., who has been active for years in the Medjugorje Movement, was interviewed by Caritas of Birmingham regarding television, his giving it up, and why.

Question: *Do you think television is dangerous for the family structure? We've gone thousands of years without something like this. Then suddenly this comes on man's horizon and forms his whole thought pattern and his opinions. It's actually a direction and, of course, a direction in a spiritual sense as a* *spiritual director would direct. Could this be something that's just too dangerous to have within the family? In other words, families for thousands of years had to deal with boredom, had to deal with what they were going to do in the evening, and now we've got this...*

Father: *Right. You don't have the social events. What I experienced in my own life immediately, when I made the decision, back in the fall of '84, that television couldn't be my habitual way of winding down at night, — I suddenly had all kinds of time to do some good reading, to talk with people that I never had a chance to before. It was just a whole different quality of life, which began to develop almost overnight, to say nothing about the five or six years later when I began to reflect back on what effects this had had on my life. I singled out three primary areas that I think*

*are destroying our culture, certainly here in
America.*

1. *Materialism was one. I noticed without being hunted by ads and the commercialism that
makes you want this and want that, whether
you need it or not, that I don't go to the store
anymore. I only go when I absolutely have to.
I find that if I put things down on a shopping
list, about half of them I erase a couple of days
later, wondering why I even put them down!
And I've gotten a detachment from things. I've
given away a number of things that I had to
others who could either use them or put them
to a worthy cause. And I'm not as bothered
now when I lose something, as I was ten years
ago; so, that whole aspect just really affirmed
to me the material thing.*

2. *Then there's the whole sexual revolution in
our day, and I just found my own life was
just being destroyed by sexual fantasies that*

*would come up totally unexpectedly because
they were imprinted through television or the
movies of our day. I got away from television;
I found that my mind, kind of, gradually was
relieved of these things. It took several years,
but it did lessen and more peace came. I just
found a whole, more wholesome, true way of
life began to develop with a lot of peace. I was
not hassled all the time with disturbing images
that, unfortunately, got recorded in the past,
but I try to keep away from them now.*

3.   *The third key area that I find prevalent in our
American culture that was affecting my life
was (I'll use the old traditional word) PRIDE,
or the American heresy — you're #1, have it
your way…. All our advertising is focused
on the glorification of the individual — and I
just found that that whole aspect, too, began
to soften in my own life so I'm much more,
let's say, at peace. I find that I don't need to put*

myself forward as I found I was prompted to do in the past. If things work out, fine. If they don't, I find the Lord opens other doors, but that "pulling oneself up by your own boot-straps" mentality and "having it your way," is kind of sick in our society.[19]

"It is time we hear from our Church on the great danger of television. It is destroying our minds, our faith, our families, our children."

A letter from

Port Washington,
New York

CHAPTER NINE

**If Saints Are Made So By The Church
Because They Live The Spirit Of Truth, Are
Their Words Not Also To Be Accepted As
The Spirit Of Truth?**

W hat do the saints who lived before and during
the era of television tell us?

Padre Pio was disturbed and disgusted by
television. He realized it would destroy family life and told everyone not to buy one. Regarding cinema or one might say, "sin"ema,
he always gave the same answer: *"The devil
is in it."* Could it be that a man whom the
world recognized as extremely holy, who
heard countless souls in confession and

would tell them sins omitted, could also have correct discernment about television?

What does television do to us? What will happen when we watch it? Amazingly, you can go back approximately 17 centuries to what St. Augustine wrote and which rings more strongly in truth today than it possibly did then. Saint Augustine (354–430 A.D.):

"The affection I had for shows and the theater had been the cause of my continual indulgence in sensuality; and I always came away more unchaste than when I entered because what one sees or what one hears excites bad thoughts, seduces the mind, and corrupts the heart." [20]

St. Cyprian (200–258 A.D.) states:

"Theaters are a school of impurity and a place where modesty is prostituted." [21]

During the time of ancient Bishop Salvian of Marseilles of France:

"It was the custom at the Sacrament of Baptism to make an extra renunciation; namely, a promise to 'avoid' going to theaters." [22]

St. John Chrysostom's (347–407 A.D.) belief was:

"He wished that all would fly from theaters as from a plague." [23]

Tertullian (Third Century), in his book, <u>Spectacles</u>, states:

"Christian religion has an extreme aversion to all sorts of public amusement and the Church abhors them and Christianity cannot, in any way, approve of them." [24]

It's amazing. These ancient saints and Christians actually speak more clearly of today's media than anything said in the present time.

So many have the attitude: everybody has
it, everybody watches it, how can it be that wrong?
Nuns watch it! Priests watch it! This wide acceptance of this medium does not make it right, nor
does it reduce our accountability. We will have to
answer to God for our sins, which television can
cause. Moral truth of five hundred years ago is the
same today, and while television has desensitized
us to these things, we will still be held accountable.
Hasn't Jesus told His followers: *"You've heard of
the sin of adultery. I tell you whoever allows it in
his heart, commits the sin."* Doesn't TV constantly
put in front of us occasions to sin? A man is a fool
to think he can sit in front of it and not be affected
by it — whatever is on. In <u>Airwaves From Hell</u>, the
priest/author states:

> *"Unfortunately, so many have succumbed to
> the 'everybody is doing it' mentality that it is
> hard to convince them that, yet, temptations
> of all kinds are bombarding 'senses' through*

this medium, the most popular, prevalent, and easily accessible form of seriously sinful entertainment." [25]

American Saint Elizabeth Seton had a vision she couldn't understand in the middle 1800s:

"Every American would have a black box in their home through which the devil would enter." [26]

This one statement by Saint Elizabeth, being who she is, a declared saint of the Church, should strike the heart as lightning in exposing the black box. Go to any outlet store and look at hundreds of those black boxes destined for the home and reflect on whether this American saint is wrong about the devil entering the home through it.

Pope Pius XII makes a prophetic and profound statement about television (in the days of Ozzie and Harriet) about the home that substantiates Saint Elizabeth Seton's prophecy. Pope Pius XII states:

"Everyone knows well that very often children can avoid the transient of attack of a disease outside their home, but cannot escape it when it lurks in the home itself. It is <u>wrong</u> to introduce risk in any form into the sanctity of the home surroundings." [27]

We should be stunned by these words, as well as Saint Elizabeth Seton's; that we have become so desensitized that we no longer see the eternal damaging danger in the sanctity of home. <u>This is a pope speaking.</u> <u>It is a saint speaking.</u> Have times changed? As you have already read, during Lent, 1996, Pope John Paul II made headline news from his balcony in the Vatican as he called for everyone to turn off their televisions for Lent.[28] Almost no one listened because the world, and those who are of it, prefer lies to truth.

A great orator of the Third Century, Lanetantius, writes:

*"I know not where you will find more cor-
ruption and vice than in a theater. Beautiful
language causes sin to appear charming. Fine
poetry and a pleasing delivery seduces the
mind and leads it as it wills."* [29]

Father Jozo, parish priest at the beginning of
the apparitions in Medjugorje, presently tells pilgrims repeatedly:

*"Get rid of your idols; destroy them through
prayer and fasting; replace the TV with an al-
tar, put the Bible on it; get rid of the mountains
of newspapers and magazines, all the human
words, and listen to God; give yourself time to
read His words."*

Again Fr. Jozo said on August 18, 1996:

*"The television, especially commercials, is
the most destructive thing that has ever come
against man."* [30]

Father Rene Laurentin, the renowned theologian, who has presented much evidence to the
Vatican regarding Medjugorje, states:

*"Television: The same principle applies to the
artificial desires created by our civilization:
'You should also abstain from television,' the
Virgin advised, according to Jelena (the inner-
locutionist from Medjugorje).*

*"This abstention can only be beneficial. It
would give an opportunity for silence and
openness to God. <u>Anyone who is in love will
find the time for love. If we love God we will
find the time for prayer. We have to borrow
the time from elsewhere. Why not take the
time that is uselessly spent in the mediocre
activity of cultivating the television set</u>, an
activity that helps us '<u>avoid silence</u>,' and papers over the hidden sorrows and the anguish
in our hearts. God is the remedy, the way to
overcome it, the solution: not a stopgap solu-*

*tion, for we who are made by God can find
our fulfillment only in him."* [31]

What we listen to and to whom we give our
ear is important. Even in Medjugorje, TV invaded
with full force. Some women spend part of their
day watching American soap operas. One woman,
losing sight of reality, went to pay a stipend for a
Mass at St. James Church so a soap-opera couple
who broke up could get back together. It is important not only to protect the eye but also the ear.
Who has ours? St. Francis De Sales spoke of giving
importance to what or whom we incline our ears:

*"From time immemorial, women have worn
earrings, particularly, no doubt, for the pleasure of their tinkling. Scripture says that Isaac
offered some to the chaste Rebekah as a first
pledge of his love. This has a mystical meaning.
The ear is the first thing that a husband should
take possession of in his wife and that a wife
must keep for her husband alone. Nothing but*

the sweet music of chaste words ought to enter it. Therefore, remember always that if the body is poisoned through the mouth, the heart is poisoned through the ear." [32]

How many wives give their ear, not to their husbands, but to empty words from daily talk shows' advice, soap operas, or those people who are influenced by them; all of which form them not toward their husbands but toward what they hear and see. The husband's ear tuned to the game on the box, in turn, tunes the wife out. He is not able, then, to take possession of her ear. It is dangerous to give the TV a center position in the family, even in a small way. If done, there will be a loss of peace and disruption in the family unit. The family is then destined to spin apart, because the center has no grace to hold it together. The TV, being a "center" for the family, impacts and directs it as a shepherd leading sheep. However, the shepherd of the family is the father, not the TV; and he is ordained by

God to lead it. This not only holds true for family life but also for religious communities. When a TV is put in their home or center, it is destined to fly apart because this medium, as a center, has no grace, cannot hold, and anarchy follows. In Father Al Winshman's interview, he was asked:

Question: *Father, we get a lot of mail, and a lot of nuns have written us over the years. Many of them are from orders that are in deep trouble, disbanding, or breaking apart. Television is always mentioned somewhere in their letters. There's frequent watching of television in their orders and they are losing community life, a lot of it, because they are watching TV every night.*

Father: *Yes, there isn't community life. I haven't experienced a deep community life, myself, in years. I have to make it myself. I'm afraid we're losing it in the modern age with the priests and the nuns. They're not identified* *as such in public, and, unfortunately, many of them are hooked on these American ways. I can't go places with some of my own brothers at times, because I disapprove of the amusements in which they participate. And I say, "This isn't right," but they say, "Oh, it's not going to bother anyone."* [33]

Father Al Lauer, a diocesan priest of the Archdiocese of Cincinnati, in his booklet, "The Bible on Sex," says:

"Also, until we shut off or throw out the TV, we'll probably never be free from extreme sexual temptations. What used to be called pornography is now prime time TV. We can't expose ourselves to garbage without constantly smelling the stench. We can't watch TV without the constant smell of sexual temptation." [34]

"Your latest book really opened my eyes. I quit watching TV shows for Lent this year and never went back. But now I understand that the real culprit is the 'box' itself. So out go all the video tapes and the box."

A letter from
Racine, Wisconsin

CHAPTER TEN

The Truth From Those In The Industry About The Medium

We have mentioned Our Lady's messages, what the saints and priests have had to say, but what about TV's own promoters — people who helped build the industry? What do some of them think?

Marshall McLuhan, professor at the University of Toronto, known as **the high-priest-philosopher** of TV and quoted in almost every source where TV is concerned, from his books has made known the statement:

*"The medium is **the** message" (medium meaning television).*

He says it's not so much the content which shapes people, but the medium itself. **At this point in these writings this may be difficult to understand that the box, the television itself, shapes people.** However, this astounding revelation will be made clearer to you once you've read further. The point now, however, is that bearing this in mind, the fact that the TV itself shapes people, not necessarily what is shown, gives more evidence of its being the Piper's pipe to seduce man during this century. He also has observed that *the "mass **media** of today are turning the world into a 'global village,' shrinking the globe with respect to shared experiences and passing new ideals or experiences to every individual on earth."*[35] This, of course, fits perfectly the bad apple principle of satan's plan and the necessity for networking people together.

We are led to sin many times by temptations which are used by being brought up from stored memories, which many times have been put there, or stamped there, by what we've seen, in order to lead us to sin during the present or future. Is this diabolical?

Ron Miller, National Syndicated TV critic says:

"As we enter an era of computerized technology that threatens to make TV an ever-more-passive part of our lives than it is now, it is frightful to imagine that somebody might be hatching some <u>diabolical new plan to manipulate our stored memories.</u>"[36]

Martin Esslin who has had a life's career in TV states that in the future, 100 to 200 years from now, the greatest disaster of the 20th Century may well be "American television."

Irving Settel writes:

"One fact is clear: because of television's impact, the world will never be the same again. Our future has been set on a new course in

every respect imaginable, in every social insti-
tution, custom, belief, or set of values. "[37]

Are we to be pleased with television? By its own people, it is stated that it is changing every custom, belief and value! Statistics and breakups give evidence to what sort of change has happened.

Newton H. Minow, head of the Federal Communication Commission, which regulates TV, etc., spoke to the National Association of Broadcasters in Washington, saying:

"I invite you to sit down in front of your
television set when your station goes on the
air and stay there without a book, magazine,
newspaper, profit and loss sheet, or rating
book to distract you and keep your eyes
glued to that set until the station signs off. I
can assure you that you will observe a vast
wasteland.

"You will see a procession of game shows,

violence, audience participation shows, formula

comedies about totally unbelievable families,

blood and thunder, mayhem, violence, sadism,

murder, Western bad men, Western good men,

private eyes, gangsters, more violence — and

cartoons. And, endlessly, commercials — many

screaming, cajoling, and offending. And most

of all, boredom. True, you will see a few things

you will enjoy. But they will be very, very few.

And if you think I exaggerate, try it." [38]

The view he expressed probably would not
surprise anyone; however, it is a shock to learn that
Newton H. Minow said the above in 1961! He was
appointed by President Kennedy and, during that
time, the TV was like Disneyland compared to now.
His insight and truth about TV, as a vast wasteland,
caused him to be replaced. **This action (his being
fired) in itself speaks of the power the medium has
in not ever being able to speak against it.**

What about science? What does it tell us regarding television? The most frightful uncovering of what the TV *really* is, fortunately, is now being exposed by scientists. After learning about it, one is able to understand to a much deeper depth why Our Lady says to **renounce and avoid it.**

"Thank you for the book on TV. It is all true and may thousands come to read this; believe it; and get rid of the box of misery!

"I have been telling my husband and children for twenty years most of what is in this book. Of course, no one was interested and our family paid the price with suffering brought on by the devil's medium."

CHAPTER ELEVEN

The Uncovering Of The Medium
What Does Science Reveal?

B efore television, communication took place in
an orderly sequence of words; then through mental
steps, plus recall of past experiences while listening
or reading, you would come to a conclusion. It was
logic. For example, an apple has a stem, it is semi-
round, red, thin peeling on the outside, with seeds in
its core. To listen to or read this statement, you go
through mental steps. Your brain analyzes each step
and puts together a mental picture from them, which
you conclude from what you heard, and also from
past experiences concerning apples that are already
stored in your memory. You had to be alert, in a state
of attentiveness. What science has found and proven
is that television skips most of these steps in the brain,

and it is just there in image. Because the image of an
event is infinitely closer to reality than any written
or spoken account, television has a way of becoming more real than life itself.[39] Something happens
that is different when you see a movie on television,
as opposed to reading the book. The book requires
your effort, and when read, it is always better than the
movie. Watching it on television you are passive, limit-
ing your imagination to what you see. Understanding
this is important to realize what the TV actually does
to you when you watch it. The following paragraph,
highlighted in bold print, is very important to grasp
before going further and should be read several times
until <u>fully</u> grasped. Before the following is read, it is
important to pray, from the heart, to the Holy Spirit
regarding what you are about to read about science
and what TV does.

**Researcher, Herbert Krugman, wanted to find
out what happens to the brain of a person watching TV. Monitoring subjects' brain waves, he found**

repeatedly that within about 30 seconds the beta
waves which indicate alert and conscious attention
change to alpha waves which indicate lack of focus
and lack of attention; the state of aimless fantasy
and daydreaming which is below the state of alert
consciousness. When given something to read, beta
waves reappeared. What surprised Krugman the
most was how rapidly the alpha state emerged. Sur-
prisingly, more research proved just as astounding:
the left side of the brain is the side that accepted the
step you just read about the description of the apple.
It processes the information and critically analyzes it.
The right side of the brain forms the images of what
you think or see, receives information emotionally,
and does not critically analyze it, leaving that job
to the left side. The right side is where images are
formed. It perceives the world in terms of moods,
sensations, feelings, starts to form an image and is
dependent on the left side to analyze and logically
help it to form the image. Krugman concluded, "the

brain responds to the medium or television, not the content difference." In other words, the "medium," the "thing" causes the left side (beta) of the brain, which defends your thoughts, your values, to <u>tune out</u>, bypassing your logical reasoning process, going straight to the right side (alpha) which contains all the feelings and sensations to implant, prompt, stamp, or mark an image in your mind and which can be made use of in temptations. Krugman, along with other researchers, has found that watching television tends to shut down the left side,[40] thereby disengaging the information processing of this area of the brain. Krugman concluded:

> *"What you receive on TV is not thought about at the time you see it."*

If you were out in a park and a bad thought or image came upon you, as a Christian or just someone with moral values, you undoubtedly will try and cast it aside lest you sin. This is a temptation. To do this, you need both sides of your brain

to process and analyze what the emotional side
receives to conclude that this is wrong. If you keep
the bad thought there and entertain it, you commit
sin. The medium shuts down your alertness and
full consciousness, processing information for you,
which is presented in a ready-made image. The
medium itself delivers the content directly to your
mind, bypassing your protective guard of critical
analysis and delivers you right into entertaining
what you see because you are **not able to think at
the time of exposure what it is you are entertaining.**
Perhaps this is why Our Lady said:

May 25, 1987

> **"...You are ready to commit sin and
> to put yourselves in the hands of satan
> without reflecting..."**

You cannot reflect because watching TV puts you
in a position of readiness for sin, an occasion for sin.
There is no ability to reason and reflect and defeat a

<u>temptation if it is already presented to you and you
entertained it.</u> How many of us have seen scenes,
bedroom scenes or lewd conduct, and watched for
two minutes. If a temptation comes upon us with
the same thoughts, and if we don't immediately
reject them, then we entertain the lewd thoughts. It
is the Church and the Holy Scriptures which teach
us that entertaining bad thoughts or images is sin.
Just as Jesus said in the Scriptures, ***"You have heard
of the sin of adultery. I tell you, he who commits
it in the heart has committed the sin."*** If, therefore,
it is a fact that the entertainment of adultery, or any
other lewd or evil action, is a sin if committed in the
heart, why then wouldn't something which is more
than a thought, which causes us to savor and entertain a lewd thought, not also be a sin? Soap operas,
commercials, and a host of other shows contain a
multitude of things that entertain the heart and
thoughts that are in constant violation of God's
precepts, holiness, and purity. Science proves we are
below the threshold of consciousness when watch-

ing television. Can you use the excuse you didn't
sin because you were not fully conscious, when you
consciously put yourself in front of the TV, knowing
from past experiences that it leads to sin?

Continuing the above message, Our Lady's
next sentence (below) clearly relates that we have
to be alert to choose God, protect ourselves, and
not allow the television to put us in this state of
unconsciously following satan because we have no
ability to reflect because of the way the medium
delivers us into evil.

May 25, 1987

> **"...You are ready to commit sin and
> to put yourselves in the hands of satan
> without reflecting. I call on each of
> you to <u>consciously</u> decide for God and
> against satan..."**

How can we claim to consciously decide for
God if we place ourselves in a dangerous position, in

which a "medium" stops our ability to be fully conscious, and gives us no other possibility but to bring us
to the occasion of sin, and even to entertain sin at the
medium's will? To watch it, we must ask ourselves,
"Are we deciding for satan?" You cannot know what
is coming or what thought or image will be thrown
upon you in the next moment, and once you do know,
you will have already entertained the lewd behavior
which, if you continue, will lead you further into sin.
But you do continue because what you have time to
reflect on is what you've seen moments before not
what you see in the present moment, and that is if
you stop at all because the medium does not allow
you to reflect. It carries you immediately to other
variations or scenes. So what you see has entered you
and you anticipate the images coming up. This makes
it impossible to protect yourself, except to completely
remove yourself from the TV.

Is it possible that the **angel of light, lucifer,**
places just beneath our noses something so com-

mon to seduce us? This something is so common, yet reaches people of all walks, even those who cannot read. Settel writes:

> *"In contrast to the written word, television knows no illiterates. Tiny children understand what they view on the home screen, even cats and dogs seem fascinated. Communication via TV is both instantaneous and complete. **For the first time since Genesis,** man has the power to reach deep into the senses of all his fellows everywhere, with the speed of light."* [41]

The way the television works is unlike any other "medium" which exists. It is a deception "itself!" We think it's the content which comes across that informs us and even directs us; however, the medium, the television, the thing, the black box, whatever you call it, actually does something to us. It is why McLuhan says:

> *"The medium is the message."*

This is difficult to understand. How is it that the TV is the message, not necessarily the content? The following may help you to see it more clearly and should be read several times, if not clear, before reading the rest of the text until it is understood.

What you see on TV when you look at it is one small dot of light, less than the size of a pinhead.[42] **That's all, a single dot which is sent from its source, network, studio, etc. as an electrical impulse. If you could freeze the screen in a microsecond of time, the only visible thing would be this single dot. When it disappears, the next "single" dot appears — only one at a time. You remember where the last dot was and are watching the present dot and you are waiting and anticipating the next dot. No images are _ever_, _ever_ there. You remember previous dots and hold them in the right side of your brain where the image is built and stamped in you. You _never_, _never_ see an image; it is not**

sent through a wire or airwaves. It is made up
in your very self, in your own mind, and all below your conscious awareness, all in a fraction
of time. This medium deceives us and it, in
itself, gets us to create in ourselves the images[43]
it dictates. The television itself does this to us,
actually putting the left side of our brain into
semi-dormancy and sneaking in and stamping
an image on the right side. This is why it is said
that the "medium (television) is the message,"
it's not the contents. The television entrances
you and seduces you by its dictates and entertains the tendency to sin by actually forming the image, perhaps in somewhat the same
way a temptation comes upon you, "except"
the television continues to lead your thoughts
which in turn will lead your heart. To subject
yourself to this medium is very dangerous to
not only the spiritual life, but also to the soul
itself. The content can be anything and satan

has never had a problem finding bad apples to mix with good apples (religious or secular program content). The real message is the box. You fill in the motion and the picture. You are very involved, very busy, and all this activity is only on one side of the brain; the left side is tuned out. This frees up the right side to accept and act upon suggestions, even commands. Simply put, you open your consciousness up to suggestions and even commands of the contents [44] which is controlled and planted in you by the medium itself.

Perhaps this is why in the beginning days of TV, thoughtful men were frightened by it because their spirits sensed what their intelligence could not. Good, bad, religious, or secular content does not matter, it is the medium itself that is dangerous.

Who controls this media/medium? Even McLuhan, whom the TV Industry adopted as their high priest, after realizing how this medium works,

ended his career [45] **because of the research about the right and left side of the brain and the process of the way dots, called electronic scanning, affect our minds. Amazingly, McLuhan, the philosopher, the high priest who helped build the TV industry, urged everyone to "pull the plug" on television because he considered it deeply violent in its effects on the mind and body!**

It is important to note that it is not the Community of Caritas of Birmingham, nor this author, but the industry itself, or people associated with it, who have discovered these things and fully believe them. Christians would be ridiculed to suggest that the TV is some kind of god. Yet, McLuhan recognized:

> *"Television is like the traditional concept of God whose "center" is everywhere and whose margins are nowhere. All seeing, omniscient, all pervasive, all-encompassing, television comforts us in our loneliness and is always*

there in our time of need, ministering and giv-
ing unceasingly, for free." [46]

Tony Schwartz, author of <u>Media</u> states: "Ask anyone raised in the religious traditions of the Western World to describe God and this would be the answer:

"God is all-knowing and all powerful. He is
a spirit, not a body and He exists both outside
us and within us. God is always with us be-
cause He is everywhere. We can never fully
understand Him because He works in mysteri-
ous ways. In broad terms, this describes the
God of our Fathers but it also describes the
electronic medium, the second god." [47]

Could it be possible that perhaps Christians are the last to understand what many of the industry themselves believe? Is it possible that with the separation of the right and left side of the brain that the Will of God would be clouded or too difficult to discern? To discern and know what is right requires rational, analytical thought and reason. One person shared that she sometimes thought she had a vocation, but she had difficulty discerning. She completely stopped watching TV, listening to the radio, and using other media. She began to strongly sense a vocation, and she finally heard the call and was sure. Does it not stand to reason that those "Divine commands" from God are clouded and interfered with when the left side of our brain is shut down or dulled into inactivity through television? At the point of no longer hearing God's commands, whose commands do we hear? Abstinence from this medium give us the ability to think more clearly and to discern more correctly.

"There was no doubt about it; my father was very much a family man. But there were two shows that he watched on TV that we did not dare to interrupt. We had to be silent."

A letter from
Springfield, Illinois

CHAPTER TWELVE

Sounds of Silence

Writer, Joyce Nelson, states:

"We are in danger of collectively responding to the god-like promptings of media echoes in the right hemisphere (of the brain) as though they were our own volition (decision)." [48]

It seems that television has become a god over many people, even unsuspecting Christians; however, we should be the first to know and yet we understand little in comparison to secular sources.

Media advisor, Jerry Grafstien, said in March, 1983:

"Television is god." [49]

These people really believe that this is a god because it can suggest and command people in an "anti" way.

God does this in our inner hearts, through our reason, by "divine promptings" (inspiration).

In the year 40 BC, a pagan named Publius Verquil spoke of a divinely-born child to come who would bring peace to the world and a new age. He described this event as one centered on a smiling, infant son whose cradle was a cornucopia of flowers and whose birth would bring about freedom from fear for animals and mankind. Jesus fulfilled this prophecy. Many times in history souls, even pagans, have received prophetic understandings about different events in history. Music of the fifty's, sixty's, and later spoke prophetic truths of today. At the time they were written, there was no understanding of what they now are revealing to us, as the following song shows:

THE SOUND OF SILENCE
(Simon and Garfunkel)

Hello darkness my old friend,
I've come to talk with you again.

Because a vision softly creeping,

Left its seed while I was sleeping,

And the vision that was planted in my brain

Still remains within the sound of silence.

In restless dreams I walked alone,

Narrow streets of cobblestone.

Beneath a halo of a street lamp,

I turned my collar to the cold and damp,

When my eyes were stabbed by the flash of a neon light,

It split the night and touched the sound of silence.

And in the naked light I saw,

Ten thousand people maybe more.

People talking without speaking.

People hearing without listening.

People writing songs that voices never shared,

No one dared disturb the sound of silence.

Fools, said I, you do not know,

Silence like a cancer grows.

Hear my words that I might teach you.

Take my arms that I might reach you,
But my words like silent raindrops fell,
Echoed in a world of silence.

And the people bowed and prayed,
To the neon god they made,
And the sign flashed out its warning,
In the words that it was forming,
And the sign said the words of the prophets are written
on the subway walls and tenement halls,
whisper the sound of silence.

The darkness of TV has become a friend
to many in their loneliness, softly creeping, placing images that form as a seed grows while one is
in the daydream state of sleepiness — planting its
vision in your brain, all in the deception of silence.
The TV's most active time is in the night, stabbing
the eye by its neon light. It hides and soothes over
the cold and damp feeling of loneliness with sound
which is not human, rather manufactured. When
exposed in naked light, multitudes talk, yet do not

really speak in the flesh; they seem to hear but do not. Thoughts you have or songs you hear while watching TV are never shared because the medium keeps you mesmerized. No one dares to <u>interrupt the sound of silence of those loved ones present in the room with you</u>, who themselves do not want to be talked to while being stabbed in the eye. Family and friends become fools sitting together in silence while sounds blare all around — a real sound of silence of no communication between loved ones. Silence like a cancer grows.

But Our Lady calls us, *"Hear my words that I might teach you; take my arms that I might reach you."* Alas, She says, *"But my words like silent raindrops fell; echoed in a world of silence."* Our Lady's words cannot enter the home of a family "silenced" by the sounds of TV. But it is what the people want, for the people bowed and prayed to the neon god they made. AND the sign flashed out its warning, in its <u>own</u> words that it was forming. False prophets' words of filth that one finds on subway walls and building halls counter the words of Our Lady. *"The sign said the words of the prophets are written on the subway walls and tenement halls, whisper the sound of silence...,"* a sound so silent, it is deafening to all who hear it, killing the social exchange between one human and another.

Pause and reread now the words of the song. Its meaning will be clearer and more prophetic to you.

How can Our Lady penetrate the silence caused by so much sound? We must be willing to turn away from that which makes death seem life and life seem death. The remainder of this chapter will prove this point.

To use Our Lady's words, **another "uncovering of deception"** and another piece of evidence is that everything that has life has a presence, an aura, something that dead things don't have.[50] Evil desires to kill life and effectively does so with the television, not the contents but the very medium itself. The television eliminates "aura" and displays death as appealing! It conveys realistic images but cannot capture the aura of something living. Living things, the way God created them, become less when viewed through television.

Jerry Mander author of <u>Four Arguments for the Elimination of Television</u>, tells:

"(Regarding his work) ... *with the Sierra Club to shoot images of the Redwood Forest in order to help them establish Redwood National Park. The footage he brought back just didn't work. It didn't capture at all the live redwoods and was flat and conveying nothing of the mood of actually being there and the splendor. Mander decided to go back and shoot again. This time, however, he shot acres of dead redwood stumps. The images of the stumps were more powerful than the living trees.*

"Without aura, the image of a living being is lifeless, merely a detailed husk of an exterior surface. The image may be entirely realistic, 'life-like,' indeed, but what it conveys is nothing more than husk or shell. That means, he says, that communication through TV of dead imagery or non-alive imagery is more efficient than communication of living imagery. Since dead objects (advertised products, a machine, or corpse) have no aura in the first place, it loses nothing in the process of being translated into an image but the living thing loses its most important quality which is life essence…. So television (not the content) accomplishes something that in real life would be impossible, making products more alive than people." [51]

This anti-human medium that makes a can of soup dance across the table, gives something without life, life. Real life is diminished, making it less than it actually is. This follows satan's desire —

death for mankind, nature, or all life on our planet.

Our Lady warns us and reveals his intent:

January 25, 1991

> **"...satan is strong and wishes not only
> to destroy human life but also nature
> and the planet on which you live..."**

Our Lady clearly states satan's plans, his "desires." Is it coincidental that <u>television</u> does and promotes what the above message of Our Lady states? The present attraction by the world to spiritual death is obvious. It should be even more apparent that a real spiritual medium is spiritually directing it. Prophets of evil predicted plans to make the dead living. This is in line with satan's false promise, *"follow me and you'll live forever,"* which is always death. Before the turn of this century, a press report, November 29, 1881, stated:

> *"The ghost will walk (speaking of photography) and that's how, little by little, science,*

progressing with giant steps, will succeed in abolishing death, its sole obstacle and only enemy." [52]

Another press quotation from the year 1875, speaks prophetically of the time coming of the life the medium will give us:

"When at last color photography has been achieved and when phonograph has been added to that, then movement and speech will be caught simultaneously with vigorous accuracy, that is to say, life itself. When that day has come — and it's coming tomorrow — science will have given us the complete illusion of life. Why shouldn't it be capable of giving us life itself?" [53]

"After reading this book so many things made sense...for example: when I was a school teacher, there were students who were 'zombies' in my class. One boy in particular sat there with a glazed look. He told me he watched TV from the minute he got home until he went to bed at night....so sad for a third grader."

A letter from
Fort Collins, Colorado

CHAPTER THIRTEEN

The Education Myth

So science uncovers the evils of TV, but what of the uses of TV for good purposes? What of using television for educational purposes? A study of half a million sixth through twelfth graders in 1980 showed: the more TV, the lower the achievement, regardless of the number of hours spent doing homework and reading.[54] A prevalent philosophy is that TV works against the education of a child. The right/left brain phenomena is enough to tell us that in a daydream state one does not learn. There is a great deal of other research that supports that TV does not educate; and rather than teaching, it entertains and actually damages a teacher's ability to compete! Teaching vs. entertaining. While we will not go deeply into it, a good deal of research is

easily available that TV does not educate; it entertains and in the long run harms one's ability to be
educated.

In Joan Anderson Wilkins' book, <u>Breaking
the TV Habit</u>, she writes:

> *"Have you ever really looked at a child in
> front of the tube? The poor thing looks like
> he's had the child knocked out of him. It is
> unnatural for a child to be anything but active
> and busy."* [55]

We, at Caritas, have seen in real life experiences what really happens when the TV and videos
go out the door. Our children suddenly had to be
creative. Their boredom was healthy because it
fostered creativity. Suddenly joy and real laughter
were heard coming from their hearts, rather than a
devious chuckle because of the TV. Their innocence
is being protected. They are being allowed to just
be kids. They play. Really play. We've seen for our-

selves that TV, aside from its other evils, diminishes
children's ability to play and amuse themselves.
In May 1994, 25 **liberals**, physicians and psycholo-
gists in England, sent a shock wave through their
whole country. They signed a statement declaring
that mistakes have been made in not protecting
children's innocence. Other liberals and the media
were outraged. It reads:

> *"Many of us hold our liberal ideals of free-*
> *dom of expression dear, but now begin to feel*
> *that we were naive in our failure to predict*
> *the extent of damaging material and its all-*
> *too-free availability to children. By restrict-*
> *ing such material from home viewing, society*
> *must take on a necessary responsibility in*
> *protecting children from this, as from other*
> *forms of child abuse."* [56]

Aside from the medium and its damage,
what about supposedly "good" contents of kids'
shows like Walt Disney's "The Lion King?" It is

no secret that there has been a gravitation of individuals over the last decades who have influenced the television and movie industry. Many of them and their lifestyles contradict, in every way, Christian precepts. Their ideals, many perverse, show up infiltrating their productions, hidden or in the open. "Newsweek" reported that "The Lion King" is a "message" movie, telling us there is no need to fear strong women, and giving some wrong definitions about family and environment. One father said:

> *"To let my children see a movie, produced by people whose lives, they believe, are normal but Christianity teaches us are abominations, makes about as much sense as to let my children play with rattlesnakes. I do not want anyone, through this medium, influencing my children and defining what family, home, or the environment are, especially when they are trying to do it subtly."*

A gentleman who left the TV business, in response to a question about the type of people who work in the television industry, said:

> *"They are a special kind, typical business people living according to the laws of the jungle. If I can't get him, he'll get me! They are people filled with hatred, crooked, lying as naturally as they breathe, hypocrites, setting themselves up while setting you up, playing vicious games. The hardest thing for me was to hear the blasphemies, and words in vain."* [57]

"A few years ago my husband and I separated and my two pre-teenage boys moved in with Dad, while the two youngest stayed with me. I was blessed with the grace of two broken TV sets and continued to live without the 'box' for three years. My two teenagers decided to move back home and in my eagerness and blindness to please them, I allowed a TV to enter our home once again. I found it more difficult to stop their viewing habits and began to lose control of the little ones as well. My third son began to do very poorly in school and also began to give me many problems at home, especially with obedience and respect. I realized then that the TV was in control of my family. Only this week after reading your letter was I given the strength to return the TV (along with a copy of the book) to their father.

"Life has already improved one hundred percent. The younger children are enjoying our family time together and soon all four children will be together to enjoy this Advent Season together. It is so much easier to focus on our prayer life and to live the messages of Christ."

A Letter From
Rockledge, Florida

CHAPTER FOURTEEN

Ok, I Accept Everything Stated, I'll Only Watch Religious Broadcasting Or Tapes

What about religious programming? Benedict J. Groeschel, C.F.R., spiritual writer and Franciscan Friar of the Renewal states:

> *"If you are really growing in holiness, you wouldn't be watching TV. You'd be doing good works with the poor or praying right now. In a certain sense I'm being facetious but in another, I'm not."* (He originally said this on a religious television program.) He adds:

> *"After work, we spend a good deal of time in life being entertained. The fact is Our Lord said for every idle word that men shall utter, they shall render an account. It is probably*

equally true that for every idle word that men shall listen to they shall also render an account. So the good Christian is struggling to have his life so organized that everything he does is directed toward the Will of God and toward being a better Christian." [58]

Father Frank Poncelet goes much further and believes the television, regardless of its programs, must be thrown out. Regarding the issue of programming or **religious** broadcasts and programming, he states, it is too little too late.

"At this late hour when satan firmly controls most TV sources, individuals' and well-intentioned groups' only recourse, virtually the only effective means remaining, is to attack the instrument." He states, "When a gunman is at your door, ready to kill your family, you don't address a letter to the association he stands for or to the maker of guns. In fact, you don't even attack him — you go directly for *the instrument he is holding, the gun, in order to save your wife and children. The time for your good intention, or hope of changing those in control of the gunman's organization has obviously passed; your only recourse is to get the gun out of his hands."* [59]

To receive religious broadcasting, you have to receive many other things which come with it and which at sometime or another will be viewed. The book, <u>Air Waves from Hell,</u> addresses this argument very well, and it is recommended to be read for further answers. **Sadly the biggest defenders** are sometimes those who justify keeping something bad because of elements of good within it. satan offers the shimmer of light, or truth, which he hates, in order to gain a foothold for his voice later. On a scale weighing good for the family versus bad for the family, good is far outweighed by the bad considering: family time, prayer time, communication with each other, and the buildup of sacredness in the family. The medium really offers none of these things with any measured success. In comparison, it promotes the ruin of family with bad behavior and the breakup of family.

If parents are watching religious broadcasting, are the children there with them? Most people say that their kids are off playing in another room, etc. Does this build family — or separation? Simply put, by its own virtues, Christian programming cannot do the things secular TV does to get and hold children's attention. Yes, maybe for a short time, but eventually you will find them wanting to turn to what the networks and cable offer. "Roger Rabbit" vs. "X." It was difficult to even think of a well-known religious, children's movie to make a comparison to show a point, so we made up one and called it — "The Moon and God." "Roger Rabbit" vs. "The Moon and God." Both of these are children's movies. "Roger Rabbit," even though a cartoon, breaks many, many Christian precepts which include seduction, bad language and appearance, smart-aleck behavior, disrespect and the presentation of vices in a cute, lovable, or favorable light. "The Moon and God" includes none of the above since it is Christian. Which will your children prefer to watch? Keeping the television for perceived good reasons, knowing it is a bad medium, is courting spiritual danger and disaster for yourselves and children.

Of course, the main point some use to justify television is the content of religious programming. Can the justification be used, bearing in mind the medium and what it does to you (brain phenomena, stamping images) which is already, in itself, enough reason to sufficiently convince you what to do? Regarding content, the medium itself, through deception, violates the free will whether it be good or bad content. For those who would argue a show is good, it's religious, how is it defended since the medium (television) not the content subverts the free will?

Yes, willingly you place yourself in front of it, you do not have to do so, but once you do, the methods of the medium working in your brain have the ability to lead your thoughts, dominating you and not giving you time to think about what you are seeing at the time you are exposed to it. While it cannot be said that TV breaks the free will, its enslavement comes as close as you can get without doing so, and that in itself is dangerous and a violence to the free will God gave man. God, on the other hand, is not deceptive. You must consciously choose Him. Evil is there and good is there. He does not "snow" you to choose Him. He wants you to come to Him being aware of all the facts and in freedom. His is an invitation to follow. satan's is a command to follow. Our Lady said:

November 25, 1987

> **"…Dear children, you know that I love you immeasurably and that I desire each of you for myself but God has**

given to all a freedom which I lovingly respect and humbly submit to...”

Our Lady's saying, **“I desire each of you for myself,”** is followed by **“but,”** knowing satan desires us and will do anything — break all rules, seduce us to violate our will, and enslave us through vices, wasting time, etc. We knowingly and unknowingly give our free will to him through the medium. He will do whatever is necessary to take hold of us, while Our Lady shows us that She stands before us humbly, quietly, with great respect and submission to man's freedom. **Justifying the viewing of television and keeping it because “I will only watch religious broadcasting” must be confronted and evaluated by the truths read.** Is it possible that God, who is truth, would want you to watch religious programming, which is delivered to you through deception? By a medium which deceives? God cannot nor would not be for deception. He does not want to call us by deceptible means, but rather with our

full consciousness and love to choose him. Jesus
told the Pharisee, **"had I not come you would have
not been responsible, but because you've heard me
you are now accountable."** Now that Our Lady has
revealed truths to us about television deceptive-
ness, be it religious broadcasting or secular, we now
carry upon us the great responsibility of knowing
truth. If we choose deception, we may very well
be choosing a path just as the Pharisees did, and by
hearing Jesus' words, suddenly were held liable. We
too can no longer claim to use a deception even for
perceived good purposes, such as religious broadcasting. Do not reject this point. It correlates with
Scripture and Our Lady's words. Mirjana was told:

March 18, 1996

> **"...Accept My messages that you may
> be accepted..."**

Reading all the previous revelations, one now is
confronted with making a decision toward good or

evil. Our Lady tells us of satan's "active" plan to enslave man through "great" temptation and that this danger is through material (television, the first among things) and the world (contents on the television which presents us the world). Our Lady says:

June 25, 1989

> **"...Pray because you are in great temptation and danger because the world and material goods lead you into slavery. satan is active in this plan..."**

Even if you already have (or haven't) made up your mind, another aspect is needed to put a complete picture together in order to see in real depth what has been placed in the world during this century. The Scriptures tell us to avoid silly and suggestive talk. It says we are not even <u>to listen</u> to it for our holiness forbids it. So how can one justify a medium in which children's cartoons contain such talk?

If this century does not belong to God, and
Our Lady has told us there are evil things, and
we consider the principles of the Pied Piper and
networking the world together (the rotten apple)
— what would the instrument be? What is it that
Our Lady comes for fifteen years[*] to "uncover" and
deliver us from? Sin, yes! She said to renounce sin.
But what is the primary instrument this world offers
which leads man to sin? Why is it She is with us
to close out this century? What kind of hold does
satan have on us that God sends Our Lady to the
earth daily for over a decade? If indeed this century has been dominated by something other than
God, then would not the Book of Revelation have
insights to reveal to us about these things? Would
Revelation not relate to a time in history when the
dragon is all powerful? Why would Revelation take
place when he is much weaker? Our Lady says
satan is strong!

---

*   Refer to footnote on page 39.

January 14, 1985

"My dear children, satan is strong. He wishes with all his strength to destroy my plans. Pray only, and do not stop doing it. I will also pray to my Son so that all the plans that I have begun will be realized. Be patient and persevere in prayer. Do not permit satan to take away your courage. He works very hard in the world. Be on your guard."

"I was overwhelmed by this book. After praying, then reading it, I couldn't believe I am so blind all these years to satan's deceptions.

"My father died at home in a hospital bed of cancer in 1976. As he lay in bed, the portable TV was to his left and a crucifix on the wall to his right. Although he was heavily sedated for pain the last few weeks, he was visibly distorted and agitated at the presence of the TV. My mom finally removed it from the room, and the last two days he had his eyes fixed on the Crucifix. Can't help but think how many hospital rooms filled with terminally ill persons are forced to face satan in their last trials unable to remove him or his channel."

A letter from
Ogema, Wisconsin

CHAPTER FIFTEEN

You've Read What The Messages, Saints, Science, And The Secular Say About The Medium; But What About The Bible?

Pope John Paul said in a homily:

> *"Mary (Rev. 12) carries the features of that woman whom the Apocalypse describes...*
> *The woman, who stands at the end of the history of creation and salvation, corresponds evidently to the one about whom it is said in the first pages of the Bible that she 'is going to crush the head of the serpent.'"* [60]

Mary is referred to in the beginning of Genesis, and presently, She is with us at the end of this time of man, in the midst of this great struggle about which Apocalypse describes. In Medjugorje, Our Lady said:

August 2, 1981

"A great struggle is about to unfold.

A struggle between my Son and satan.

Human souls are at stake."

The Pope went on to say in his homily:

"She it is with whom the apocalyptic dragon
makes war, for being the Mother of the re-
deemed, She is the image of the Church whom
we likewise call Mother." [61]

When we study Revelation, it becomes evident that
Our Lady's message parallels it. Her constant call
to conversion is just what Revelation encourages. A
recent book about Revelation called The Navarre
Bible — Revelation, Text and Commentaries, states:

"The Revelation of John constitutes a strong
call to conversion. It urges people to commit
themselves to God and put their trust in God."[62]

Indeed, the Book of Revelation seems to collaborate with many events taking place. It is not to say they won't also apply sometime in the future, but Holy Scripture is living, not dead. It is multi-purpose. A verse can speak to us now regarding something, and ten years from now, it can also speak to us about something completely different.

June 25, 1991

> **"...If you pray, God will help you discover the true reason for my coming. Therefore, little children, pray and read the Sacred Scriptures so that through my coming you discover the message in Sacred Scripture for you..."**

This message was given on the tenth anniversary of Our Lady's appearances in Medjugorje. Why does Our Lady say, **"...discover the true reason for my coming"** and **"read Sacred Scripture"** to know? Why do we not already know Her true reason for coming? Surely it would seem after ten years we would know. What is it after sixteen years (as of June 1997) and hundreds of messages, we still are to discover — and in Sacred Scripture at that? Pope Pius XI speaks of self-indulgence, greed for possessions, and said:

> *"The disease of the modern age and the main source of the evils we all deplore is that "lack of reflection," that continuous and quite feverish pursuit of external things, that immoderate desire for wealth and pleasure, which gradually causes the heart to lose sight of its nobler ideals, drowning them in a sea of impermanent, earthly things, and preventing them from contemplating higher, eternal things."* [63]

Does not television exactly represent the above?

Remarkably, Pope John Paul II said, regarding the **beast** in Revelation, that aside from the interior struggles of the heart, in regard to rebel-

lion in the modern era, it (the beast) will take on
a concrete form as the **"content"** of culture and
civilization as an ideal and philosophy or a program
for action for the shaping of human behavior. The
Pope says:

> *"It reaches its clearest expression in material-*
> *ism, both in its theoretical form — as a system*
> *of thought — and in its practical form — as*
> *a method of interpreting and evaluating facts,*
> *and likewise as a programme of correspond-*
> *ing conduct."* [64]

The single "thing" which encompasses the Pope's
statement in all areas of thought and the shaping
of human behavior is TV. Our Lady's message of
March 25, 1996 fits the above like a glove:

> **"...In this time, when due to the spirit**
> **of consumerism, one forgets what it**
> **means to love and to cherish true val-**
> **ues, I invite you again, little children,**

to put God in the first place in your life…"

Unfortunately, TV is in the first place in families all over the world. It is in the first place in promoting behavior through consumerism — *"buy this; get this; desire; want; lust for; have; you deserve."* Most incredibly, Our Lady says of **"consumerism"** that it is a **"spirit."** By what She says, we know this spirit is not of God. So these questions must be posed: *"Where does this spirit dwell?" "Where does its voice cry out the loudest?" "What does it make as its first throne?"*

But how could we be so deceived? St. Cyprian writes of satan:

> *"…because he moves silently and seems peaceable and comes by easy ways and is so astute and so deceptive that he tries to have night taken for day, poison taken for medicine. So by deception of this kind, he tries to de-*

stroy truth by cunning. That is why he passes himself off as an angel of light." [65]

Perhaps then we should ask how could we not have been deceived? We quit praying. We accepted this "thing" without question. It stands to reason, a far superior and more advanced intellect could deceive us. satan is the master of deception. Who do we think we are, not praying and not living holy lives, and still expecting the intelligence and spiritual wisdom to see what the great deceiver has done? So now Our Lady comes to give us the wisdom, tell us how to obtain it and grow holy, and to reveal the evidence piece by piece. Now She leads us to Holy Scripture to learn the **"true reason for my coming."** So turning to Revelation in prayer, we began to understand. The following may seem simplistic because it is. Materialism and consumerism can be explained in volumes of complex ways; however, for common man, everything can be simplified as follows.

Revelation, Chapter 13, speaks of a beast and the "dragon" (representing satan) which gave "<u>it</u>" his own power and throne, together with great authority. satan gave this beast or "thing" his full authority to captivate the whole world, for Revelation 13 says:

> *"In wonderment the whole world*
> *would follow after the beast."*

What fits this description? Revelation 13 also says:

> *"Then I saw a wild beast come out of*
> *the sea…"*

The very first time airwaves were used, "a message" was broadcasted from a ship at sea to the shore.[66] The following is stated from a historical source:

> **"The proving ground of radio was the**
> **sea, the one part of the world which**
> **could not be reached by a wire."** [67]

It can then be said that radio came out of the sea and radio through music, useless chatter, and many other things promoted the world — lewd behavior, lust, and want. We wake up to it, get out of the shower to it, get in the car with it, jog with it, eat with it, shop with it. We virtually cannot escape it — in public stores, bathrooms, restaurants, etc. What else, before the radio, has honored satan and promoted his interests as much? Its promotion of evil, no one can stop. Revelation 13:4 says:

> *"Men worshiped the dragon for giving his authority to the beast; they also worshiped the beast and said, 'Who can compare with the beast, or come forward to fight against it?'"*

Through it, disrespect toward God and constant blasphemies against Him have come upon the earth, twenty-four hours a day, non-stop. Verse 5 says:

"The beast was given a mouth for
uttering proud boasts and blasphe-
mies,..."

Radio and the "medium" continue to boast about
their greatness, and it seems to become more bois-
terous as each week, month, and year pass by, not
only being content to commit blasphemies against
God, but now anything and everything holy, including His saints. Verse 6 says:

"It began to hurl blasphemies against
God, reviling Him and the members
of His Heavenly household as well."

Has any instrument of man's history fit this
description as this medium does today? And what
part has it had in influencing Christians to accept
many errors, to be plagued with many problems,
and in dominating the way we and our children
behave? Verse 7 says:

"The beast was allowed to wage war against God's people and conquer them. It was likewise granted authority over every race and people, "language" and nation."

God allowed Job to be tested. War was waged against him. Can we reasonably question whether permission was granted to try the world during this century? What kind of beast is there that could have authority over every **"language,"** let alone every "nation," "people," "race," and even enter into "God's people?" Could it be carried by airwaves to all the languages and nations? Reason and think! Isaiah says, *"Come reason with Me."* Reason, Holy Reason, based in God's word, precepts, and Church teaching can help you see light? This is something God wants you to do, but if blocked by media, you are not able to reason toward truth. Your mind is influenced and occupied. The second beast, Verse 11–15 says:

"Then I saw another wild beast come out of the earth. It had two horns like a ram, and it spoke like a dragon. It used the authority of the first beast to promote its interests by making the world and all its inhabitants wor-ship the first beast…It performed great prodigies; it could even make fire come down from Heaven to earth as men <u>looked on</u>. Because of the prodigies it was allowed to perform by authority of the first beast, "<u>it</u>" led astray the earth's inhabitants, telling them to make an idol… The second wild beast was <u>THEN PERMITTED TO GIVE LIFE TO THE BEAST'S IMAGE SO THAT THE "IMAGE" HAD THE POWER OF SPEECH…</u>"

TV's voice is transmitted through FM radio. TV's image gives life to the voice. Is there any thing or beast in history that could match this revelation so perfectly? Does John, a First Century man, describe, as best he could, man perhaps looking at TV with the screen making fire come from Heaven? Prodigy is defined as an extraordinarily marvelous or unusual accomplishment, deed or event. Man, when TV first came into use, was saying these things about this medium. In the book, A Pictorial History of Television, television is referred to as:

"Infant prodigy." [68]

It would be hard to understand how John would not be amazed at the vision he saw. All this is enough to make your skin crawl and cause disbelief, but the next verse is important also. Science has shown us that TV deceptively forces and stamps an image directly in the right side of our brain by bypassing our logical, analytical left side. Under normal reasoning conditions, the left side allows us to more easily understand God and His desires for us. The television, advertising, and associated industries universally accept the methods and end results of right/left brain phenomena and dot scanning.

Tens of millions of dollars have been poured into research to better understand how to "prompt" people into buying products or ideals. President Carter, 30 points behind in the polls, hired and paid one of the leading experts in the world on these methods to build an advertising campaign, to manipulate and prompt directly the image that he should be president. Everyone was surprised, some even shocked at how he swept into the presidency. About the only ones who were not surprised by it were those whom he hired to do just that. They knew their tactics work. There are one-hundred-million-dollar companies guided by people who understand these powerful methods and utilize them. These methods are used not only to sell products, but to buy any and everything, even political offices! More and more, everything bought or sold is beginning to come under the control of this unseen force. From the book, The Perfect Machine, is quoted:

> *"The techniques derived from knowledge of the right hemispheric (brain) processing (by the medium) and appeals is now standard procedure in political campaigns and public relations efforts."*[69]

There is so much information which proves this, that many books could be filled. It is not from the religious or extremists, but from those in the industry itself, and it is this evidence which helps us see the following. **All people of the earth, all classes, are influenced through an unseen, yet intelligent, knowing, deceptive force. This force has the ability to imprint an image on the right side of the brain and influence people to submit to "false, divine" promptings. It leads multitudes, not only toward evil, but also to buy and sell everything from food to political offices.**

Continuing, Revelation 13:16–17:

> *"<u>It</u> (beast) forced all men, small and great, rich and poor, slave and free, to accept a stamped image on their right hand or their forehead. Moreover, it did not allow a man to buy or sell anything unless he was first marked with the name of the beast…"*

An image placed in our mind that is deceptively forced upon us, without our even being fully conscious of what this medium is doing, could easily be described as a mark. Coupling all of this with Our Lady's message calling consumerism a spirit, breaks all doubts left in regard to the medium.

"THE DEVIL'S EYE" — 1979 rock song

Can you hear me, are you listening, has your programme disappeared?
I can see you, I am watching you, I've been planning this for years.
I have blacked out your television, every station in the world is mine,
And there are millions who are just like you as you sit there, paralyzed!
I have some orders which you will follow, and there's nothing you can do,
'Cos as you're looking at your TV screen, I am looking back at you…

> *Oh side by side,*
> *We will cross that Great Divide,*
> *'Cos nothing's gonna save you now from the Devil's Eye!*
> *Oh nothing's gonna save you now from the Devil's Eye…*

Turn your dial to the number that is shining on your screen,
You will notice that everything is red, you won't need blue or green,
All around me, fire is burning, yes I'm calling you from hell,
And all those people who haven't seen me yet, will soon be under my spell.
Something's happening, sounds like thunder, maybe the Lord is on His way,
He's still angry and He's after me, since I cheated on the Spanish train,
Oh yes He's coming, and He could stop me, but He'd better make it soon,
'Cos the last time that I won a world, I made it into a moon…

> *Oh side by side,*
> *We will cross that Great Divide,*
> *'Cos nothing's gonna save you now from the Devil's Eye!*
> *Oh side by side,*
> *Forever we will ride,*
> *'Cos nothing's gonna save you now from the Devil's Eye!*
> *I can see you,*
> *I can see you, I can see you…*

Sung by Chris Deborgh

170

CHAPTER SIXTEEN

Is There Any Defense Left for You Keeping the TV?

How can it be? It's not reality! Perhaps Revelation just may actually be taking place. We pinch ourselves. How could it be we're alive while these verses may be coming into play? We almost can't believe it. We want to — we don't want to. It's supposed to be off in the future somewhere — yes, maybe around the corner. But not while we're alive. We are frightened by it and excited by it — all these thoughts at the same time. This writer feels the same way. It is almost unbelievable, but Our Lady's messages reveal it. The evidence keeps coming. It is there. But logically, what other time would it be, especially if satan has this century? The Scriptures say he will give his <u>full</u> authority to

those beasts who will speak blasphemies day and
night to every man of every class on earth. Spanning the time of man, does anything fit these verses
so clearly? They meant little to man for 1900 years,
because he had no way to understand them. If John
actually saw a vision of the way TV works, the buying and selling of products and ideas, would not the
spirit of what he saw reflect that which he wrote
— man being forced and imaged on his right hand
and, moreover, not being able to buy or sell without
the mark? John says everyone who bought or sold
was marked by this beast. He may have used the
word "beast" because his mind had no understanding of mechanics and machines. Would anyone in
the First Century describe this medium as a beast?
It may have appeared to him as though it had life,
and back then, only animals or man could perform
actions on their own. So describing a "thing" as a
beast would be understandable.

We do not dare say Revelation means exactly this or that. The Church must do that, and we submit to the Church, and even defend Her right to do so. However, the Church offers little on these verses. If and when She does speak, it will possibly happen because of insight brought forth from belief or actions of many of Her members regarding a particular matter. Then the Church, through the Holy Spirit, will make a judgement and guide us. Our Lady's messages are bringing about these insights. Prophecy is not completely understood until it is fulfilled, then everything begins to become clear.

A saint, who was a nun in the late 1800s, saw herself in a vision wearing medals on her habit. She was plagued by this, did not understand, and was even sometimes troubled at its meaning. Five years later, when she attended a function in which she was a participant, military officials honored her by pinning their honorary medals on her. Although

her humility was embarrassed by their action, she
now clearly understood the vision she had had
years earlier. [70]

In Revelation, as in most prophecy for that
matter, it is this way. It cannot really be understood
fully until fulfilled. In the Revelation verses you
just read, only a few lines were cited, and some of
the ends of the verses were purposely left out. This
was not done to deceive you, but so you wouldn't
be distracted by that which is still not understood,
because perhaps it is still in the future or not completely fulfilled. What was shown was for insight
about the medium, its description, and its deception,
which Our Lady is uncovering. We tell you that
there are things left out so you know what you are
being presented, and to encourage your own judgement. For example, verse 5 said the beast was given
a mouth for uttering proud boasts and blasphemies.
That is what applied to what was being written. The
other part of the verse, which we did not include

so you would not be distracted from the point being made, was: *"...But the authority it received
was to last only forty-two months."* This, like the
nun's example, is not clear in light of present times,
perhaps because it has not been fulfilled. In past
history, early Christians ascribed this verse to Nero
and his period of persecution. This proves that
Scriptures have life, meaning the verse may apply to
present and future ages.

Another example of a part of a verse being
left out because it was unclear is: *"...the Beast suffered a mortal wound to the head..."* One can only
speculate at this point in the "present time" what
this means, because nothing applies to the "mortal
wound" unlike the case of the other verses which
provided good, clear descriptions of the medium/
media. As with the nun, it is not presently understood regarding the beast being mortally wounded
in the head, "killed," yet somehow surviving. Al-

though speculative, what is now presented is offered as an insight to what this could possibly mean.

Ivanka's apparition of June 25, 1989 took place in her living room. Those present gathered around the Crucifix which hung on her wall. Ivanka came in and prayed in preparation for Our Lady's coming. When the apparition occurred, one who was next to her observed her face closely, knowing that she was conversing with the Mother of God. He looked at her eyes and then at the wall to judge about where Our Lady was positioned, meditating on where Our Lady's eyes, Her veil, Her hands would be. Looking back to Ivanka, he felt great peace, knowing right there in front of him was the lap that Jesus sat on. He judged Her standing there, Her beauty, even though he could not see anything but a wall, but fully believing Who was before him and tracing where Her features probably were. He looked where Her feet would be, and his joy changed to a cold chill. He felt his skin crawl as though the Spirit of God came over him, for there where he judged Our Lady's feet would be was the top of the television set. The spirit of grace, giving his skin chills, spoke to him clearly — The Woman of Revelation crushing the head of the serpent!! Our Lady then gave the message we've already quoted during that apparition. It clearly can be applied first and foremost to the enslavement of TV and its offering of the world to us. The following message was given to Ivanka by Our Lady as She stood above and upon the black box on June 25, 1989:

> **"Pray because you are in great temptation and danger because the world and material goods lead you into slavery. satan is active in this plan..."**

The mortal wound to the beast's head may well be Our Lady's coming for 15 years,* Her coming to expose this beast through Her messages, the

* Refer to footnote on page 39.

necessary weight to crush him. Her messages on the 25th of each month, which surely he must dread, are to go out to every race, class, language, and nation. They are to counter the opposite voice, the image, the **"medium is the message,"** which also goes out to every race, class, language, and nation. In the last century, and now this one, this medium has been successful in attempting every blasphemy by electronic wizardry. Our Lady is coming as the Woman of Revelation (Chapter 12), with a crown of twelve stars, clothed with the sun, to do battle with the dragon. Could it be that satan is coming through the beast, making prodigies of fire come down from the sky on it, crowning himself with movie "stars" full of pride, thus "anti-ing" Our Lady's stars? Is it his message that has prevailed over man, and now Our Lady's message each month which must prevail?

The monthly message is given to Marija on the 25th of each month. Our Lady says these messages are "life" which flows once-a-month through sources. These sources are people, whom She Herself has chosen, who work worldwide spreading Her messages. The sources produce fruit as one would plant trees in different places on the Earth. Our Lady says this fruit, the "messages," which are crystal clear to Her children, are conveyed from the Throne of God. This is life-giving water being poured out as a river to the world, through all the streets, as medicine to heal the nations of the world. Our Lady produces the fruit to lead us to a time She calls "a new time," which means an end of the present time. In the end of the Book of Revelation, the last chapter of man, the end of the Bible, the very last sentences, read:

Revelation 22:1–2

> *"The angel then showed me the river of life-giving water, clear as crystal, which issued from the Throne of God and of the Lamb and flowed down*

the middle of the streets. On either
side of the river grew the trees of life
which produced fruit 12 times a year,
once each month, their leaves serve as
medicine for the nations."

So clear are Our Lady's messages to those who accept them that Revelation comes to life for us. Though dormant for centuries, now Our Lady's messages, given **once each month** on the 25th, **twelve times a year,** will be the cure, **the medicine for the nations** of the world!

If Our Lady crushes this medium, and what it entails, through people turning against it and following Her messages, will a future generation allow it to come back — survive this mortal wound to the head? We must ask ourselves what is so necessary that God sends us an intermediary daily for years, coming like an angel, if it were not for some great, historic moment for man. As the Israelites were led out of bondage, so too, Our Lady comes to free us from the bondage of sin and those evil things which lead us to sin. The message from Our Lady, which you read in the beginning of this book, said:

April 4, 1985

"...I wish to give you messages as it has never been in history from the beginning of the world..."

Could it be that we receive this grace from God, through Our Lady, because satan was allowed to **offer his message as <u>never</u> before since the beginning of man, during this century?**

All that you've read was presented to you **initially** from what Our Lady said, **secondly** from the saints, **thirdly** from secular media and the TV industry, **fourthly** from science, and **fifthly** from the Scriptures. Amazingly, these are five different sources quoted, ranging from Our Lady Herself, to scientists, Godless people, and even feminists, from various backgrounds and ideologies, that bring us to a point of decision. Perhaps it is why Our Lady continues to tell us to decide for God, because once we have understood, then there is a clear choice that must be made.

The most profound of all five groups, aside from Our Lady's messages, is that of science. It is not merely Christian belief or opinion; it is not just a few scientists who believe this medium, and not the content, is able to put an image on the right hemisphere of your brain and lead you subconsciously; but it is the whole media and industry itself. They speak of its power, and some are beginning to say it is a god. What is it, and what kind of hold does it have on us, that those who are not necessarily coming from a Christian prospective are saying, "pull the plug?"

Harvard theologian, Harvey Cox's view of mass media, is that **we should not try to use it, but try to dismantle it.**

As we stated with the detective and his example, when all the evidence is in, the picture becomes clear. From completely different sources, the pieces are put together, and we can now see why Our Lady said to **renounce television.** Could some of what is presented here be wrong? Yes, to some degree or another. But there is so much proof that the one who has given the authority to this medium has a hold over man, his direction in daily life, his actions and his role and behavior in society, that these writings are only the tip of the iceberg. What can we do? What are we to do? As the Book of Revelation states:

"Who can come against it?"

And also Revelation states:

"In wonderment, the whole world followed after the beast."

The following article, titled "The Lighter Side," was taken from the Detroit News, December 27, 1994:

> Hundreds of Bombay residents have tossed their televisions out their windows to protest violence and sex on Indian TV.
>
> It started a few months ago when Safira Alli Mohammad carried her family's set to the window of their high-rise apartment and threw it out.
>
> The tremendous crash caught the attention of nearby residents, and it soon began raining TV sets. All 1,200 families in area apartments now are reported to be TV-free.

CHAPTER SEVENTEEN

What We Can't Do and Can Do

What we can't do is react in fanaticism. <u>No one</u> should condemn another who has a TV once one decides to cast his out. Many are in a process of conversion and simply have not attained a level of spiritual understanding to grasp what this medium really does. The facts speak for themselves, and once one is presented with what is written here, he must be free to choose by his own free will that God has given him. Our Lady says:

1984 – 1985

> **"...It is necessary to respect the Commandments of God in following one's conscience..."**

A warning is necessary here because conscience and feelings are two different things. **Feelings can say yes, while conscience says no. A correct conscience must be based on God's precepts and His commandments. Then follow your conscience as Our Lady says. These writings appeal to your conscience, not to what you want or feel is correct.** Conscience, based on God's precepts, must dominate. Television by its nature appeals to your feelings. However, in the end, what one chooses to do is his right, by God's design, because He gave man intelligence and free will. God wants us to turn away from evil by choice, not force — by our love for Him. It would be fanatical for anyone to begin **demanding** others to throw away their TVs or condemn them for their use of it. Nor should you even condemn all use of it if some choose to use it. God will hold them accountable according to their knowledge. However, reading the preceding indicts those souls which have this knowledge. Being aware of its dangers, yet continuing to use television, places the soul into grave temptation and dangers. In other words, by reading these words, you are charged by the truth the words give.

What is stated is what Our Lady has shown us, here at the Community of Caritas, after years of prayer and discernment. It is quite clear where Our Lady has led us. The facts prove that anyone who has a desire for truth will come to the same conclusion. Truth has to come through invitation and enlightenment. It is Our Lady's way. Of course, parents have the right to make decisions regarding their children because they are charged with guiding them, just as the father is with guiding the family. To impose on others outside of your immediate family or those you are not charged with guiding is not Our Lady's way. It has to be done through information and based on sound doctrine, appealing to man's conscience.

What we can do is pray that Our Lady will help us realize what She is asking of us. We can pray for change in our families, in the way we do things, and in the way we live in our homes. Although a major adjustment, many are now throwing away their televisions. The TV and the family, the holy family, the close family, simply will not go together. If Mary and Joseph would have had television available during their day, does anyone think that they would allow Jesus to see it? Those who for several years have tried to live what Our Lady asks are realizing more and more where She really is leading us. We are hearing from families who are realizing the destruction which surrounds this medium, such as the following:

Dear Caritas,   *9/20/94*

"My husband and I are parents of two young children. We reached a decision concerning television that has had an impact far greater than we had hoped.

"We were trying, as good parents, to limit the exposure our children had to unsuitable pro-

*grams. Even though the programs we chose
for our children were appropriate, the advertising of other programs that our children pas-
sively witnessed was very dark in spirit. It was
our realization that it was humanly impossible
to monitor 100% of the material viewed by our
children. We realized that due to the content
of television, our children's gift of discernment
was being destroyed. They were being given a
slanted view of reality and family life.*

*"Due to the removal of television from our
home, our family life has reached new heights.
Our children's imaginations and physical play
exceed our expectations. We interact on a
deeper and more fulfilling level. We listen to
music more often as a family. We read together. We play games together. We talk. We
know each other more deeply.*

*"Our children are our gifts from God. As
parents, we have been entrusted with them and*

asked by God to lead them to holiness in life.
Television interfered with our role as parents.

"We now have more time to pray as a family,
and our life is becoming more and more ful-
filling. It is as if our vision has become crystal
clear, and we are able to experience, as well as
do, God's Will more easily. It was not easy in
the beginning to turn away from television —
yet, it was not as hard as one would expect."

Fairhope, Alabama

Our Lady called for the Year of the Family.
Every obstacle in the family's way is to be removed
if we are to experience joy and family happiness.
"Things" do not help make families happy — love
does. Two parents who love each other in their
home will be such a delight, their children will
forget the absence of television. This love will be
like being under a warm blanket for the family, and
everyone will want to snuggle under it.

"We read your book <u>I See Far</u>. After prayer and voicing our feelings/concerns, we as a family decided to give Our Lady a gift along with that of ourselves — our NEW $1200 TV and VCR! So as our consecration ended on December 8, we put a statue of the Blessed Mother on top of the TV, unplugged it, and said together three Hail Mary's. **As we were kneeling and praying in the living room, the TV <u>actually groaned</u>!** *We have a peace in our home that was felt immediately after turning <u>off</u> and <u>unplugging</u> 'the beast.'"*

A letter from
Lacome, New Hampshire

CHAPTER EIGHTEEN

Exorcism?

Our Lady used two words in Her messages specifically concerning the television: **avoid** and **renounce**. To "avoid" as you've read means: to expel, to depart or withdraw from, leave, remove, to refuse to. To "renounce" as you've also read means: *"to give up by formal declaration."* These two words show that Our Lady is asking us to expel it and formally declare ourselves and our families, in prayer and action, against it.

One father did just that, realizing more and more the bad influence of TV. One night, after the family was asleep, he prayed the following over the television:

"Father, I see no fruit coming from this thing
and as Jesus saw no fruit from the fig tree
and cursed it and it withered, I, too, curse this
'thing.'"

He did this knowing to remove it at this time would
cause a war in the family. *Two weeks later, lightning*
struck it, completely frying the insides, destroying it!

Prayer is where the family needs to begin in removing the television. No one should
expect lightning, as was the case with the father
who prayed, but you can expect God to hear your
prayers. Once you are able to expel it, you will
have fulfilled Our Lady's request of renouncing,
thereby avoiding it in the family.

A father, with his children, brought their TV
to the Field at Caritas, where Our Lady had appeared to Marija in America, and they destroyed
it. Then, in prayer, he consecrated his family to Our
Lady and by this act, turned against everything that

television offered. This was the renouncing he felt Our Lady asked for — a formal declaration. Since that first television was destroyed on the edge of the field, other families have come and destroyed their TVs, VCRs, and Nintendo machines and games also. When the families leave their TV's behind, they leave, filling the void by being attached and consecrated to Our Lady. Most of these families, feeling as they do about the medium, realize it would be a contradiction to sell it because doing so may cause someone else to fall because of it. They have chosen to set an example to their children and let them participate in formally destroying it as a family. It is a real lesson for them, and their family life becomes richer, as the previous letter has related.

Getting rid of the television may not always be so easy. To avoid and renounce the TV may be compared with the following three examples:

1. A cyst can be removed in a simple, one-day, out-patient surgery.

2. A tumor on the brain, which is serious and life threatening, may be surgically removed with patience and determination. After planning, prayer, proper order of medical steps, and necessary procedures, healing can possibly take place.

3. A tumor on the brain stem which cannot be removed and to do so would kill the patient. Living with it will eventually cause the body's malfunction and possible death, but the only hope is for a miracle through prayer.

The first example is a couple who both see the light or who, through the husband's guidance and the wife's agreement, even if she doesn't understand, decide to destroy its presence in the family. Another example is a single person who decides to remove it. It's a simple procedure with few complications. Children will adjust easily if parents are unified in their resolve.

The second is a couple whose husband wants to take it out but the wife opposes him. Even though he has the right to do so, the damage caused by his just throwing it away would be like a surgeon carelessly rushing into an operation to remove the tumor without proper x-rays and planning. He must proceed with gentleness and prayer for a month, year or even two, but eventually surgery must take place and when all other means are exhausted, the husband has the right to throw it out, even over the objection of his wife.

The third is the husband who refuses to remove it while the wife sees all the dangers. She cannot throw it out the way the husband above can, because by divine order, she has to accept the structure which God set up for the family. Hers is one of suffering and her only recourse is prayer, answered by a miracle. To badger, intimidate, and fuss would only be counter-productive, just as would a surgeon's operating on an inoperable tumor. However, with a sweet disposition and fervent prayer, God will hear the wife and change the husband's heart, through grace and her holy actions. Yes, it may take months or years, but holiness is blessed with God's answer.

Youth or teenagers will react differently according to the parents. Parents have every right to decide what goes on in the home. A family is not a democracy and children do not run a household. Parents have no difficulty enforcing the requirement that their children go to school or brush their teeth. Two unified parents will quickly mute rebellion. However, a divided response of one parent, who has the resolve, while the other does not, will foster and continue the rebellion. Unity is your key to success.

These three examples are important because the attachment to television is so strong that it is actually causing families to tear apart. Family division, in itself, is a sign of a demonic hold, but as with an **exorcism**, one may experience reactions from

family members which will shock you. Casting
out the television has caused reactions in families
no different than an exorcisms on demonics. Why
would it not be the case with its holding power and
strength over individuals of the family. A warning
of great prudence, coupled with prayer, is vital and
each situation must be evaluated. Once the television is removed, you can expect things in your life
to be very different, but not abnormal. For sixty
centuries and more, man has occupied his time
without television and that is the norm. The last 45
years with TV is abnormal, compared to man's history. Joan Anderson Wilkins, in her book, Breaking
the TV Habit, writes:

> *"Staying unplugged is not deprivation. In fact,*
> *many families report that after their decision to*
> *live without television, they feel free for the first*
> *time from the dictatorial hold television had*
> *had on their lives." She goes on, "After several*
> *years of talking to and counseling on how to*

*turn off the TV sets, I decided to go to the children themselves and began presenting '**No-TV Week.**' programs. The children participated in these programs. The children are enthusiastic and learn a great deal about the medium they once took for granted. In many cases, their parents are less excited."* [71]

When it comes down to it, children really don't want or need TV. It is the parents who teach them the habit. Children want their parents.

"Kids should run in the woods, swing from trees, swim in the creek down the road, and play 'hide and seek' half the night with the other kids in the neighborhood. My nieces and nephews sit in front of the tube with a mesmerized look that clearly shows they are below consciousness, and the images zing right into their brain with no critical thought whatsoever. One has to practically shake them out of a stupor to get them to come and eat. My brothers and sisters will not hear the words nor open their eyes to see."

A letter from
Davison, Michigan

CHAPTER NINETEEN

Are You Using the Medium to Babysit?

Parents who use the television to baby-sit their children, putting them bodily in front of it to quiet them down, do a great deal of damage to them. The camera is an eye and through this medium it will watch your children for you, making them quiet and docile. This is a very tempting thing for a parent who wants a little quiet. But parents who do this are the losers, and years down the road these decisions will produce bad fruit. Granted, there are many who do this in ignorance, but selfishness is usually the motivation. *"I'll turn the TV on so I can do my own thing or work."*

Mirjana, the visionary, said of Mary, while living upon the earth, *"Mary always put Herself*

second. She never, ever once put Her needs first."
Evidence tells us that watching TV damages children's creativity and their ability to play. They get a distorted view of reality. There is research for this.

We, at Caritas, have experienced this ourselves. Once when the adults and parents of the community were meeting, the children played for over an hour, "cutting up," imagining, noisily — but really playing with joy. They've learned to do this since we gave up TV. In our meeting, we were discussing the ills of television when we decided to conduct an experiment. One office had a TV to review tapes sent to us and all the adults gathered in that large office. One went out to tell the children simply, *"We have a movie on TV for you to watch."* They came more quickly than if we had called them to supper. We suspected what would happen but it still amazed us. Within two minutes, all the laughter was gone, all the joy had left. Their faces became serious, drone-like with no happiness shining

through. Cheerful smiles gone, they sat as if under
a witch's spell — and this was a religious movie!
Yes, there may be a laugh every now and then, but
it's not the same laugh of joy from the heart. It was
strong proof for us that what the TV philosopher,
Marshall McLuhan, said was true: *"'the medium
(television) is the message' not its contents."* Regardless of what movie we might have shown them,
the resulting damage to their childhood — their
capability of healthy play, social exchange, family
exchange — would have been the same.

Joan Anderson Wilkins writes of the outcome
in a neighborhood where a school's "No-TV Week"
was implemented:

> *"The street was full of kids, everyone doing*
> *something. The bikes were out, wagons were*
> *carting junk, basketballs were bouncing, nerf-*
> *football catching was going on the front lawn,*
> *it was like a three-ring circus. Neighborhood*
> *children needed one another more when tele-*

vision was out of the picture. It was apparent that 'No-TV Week' brought the kids together both in spirit and physically. It brought the community out of the closet and into each others' homes." She adds, "The children set up little retreats (hide-a-ways) in every corner of the house. There wasn't a blanket or sheet in the linen closet. Once inside their little retreats, the children read, talked, played with their Legos and Matchboxes and had fun. One other interesting note, the kids didn't gravitate to games. They gravitated to each other and their parents." [72]

She went on and wrote about the children picking up the hobby of reading and reading to each other.

Here is an important Bible verse to remember from Isaiah 1:18:

"Come reason with me, says the Lord."

Reason it out. What has civilized man done every night for sixty centuries? That's almost two and one half million nights. There must have been a lot of sitting around the fire. One father relates:

"I feel a fire is important to give us an incentive to gather together. I purposely turn the heat down and crank up the fire in the fireplace and then we bring out the blankets and gather around the fireplace. It brings us closer together as family, centered around the parents, instead of the TV, and we share a feeling of security. We talk and listen and sometimes just look at the fire, but we are warmed more by the love that is fostered by these actions than by the fire. Looking into the fire, we sometimes talk of all those who have gone before us, 1,000 – 2,000 years ago, and how those children sat around the fire with their fathers and mothers. Stories are told, life's lessons are taught, questions are answered. It is also

a joy to let my children work with me in cutting and gathering the wood. A great deal can be learned from it. It teaches preparation, the value of work, and all this effort comes back to me in children who are balanced and directed by me rather than by someone in Hollywood.

"I see the TV as a real, living, thief, stealing memories and joys while implanting its ideals. To keep it there is to keep a burglar in the house. Families should take the money they spend on tapes and TVs, VCRs, and entertainment and save up and install a fireplace — not a cheap one, a good one — big enough to produce heat and take up a wall, with room for gathering around it. We all fall asleep around ours. It's difficult to carry my little ones to bed every night when exhausted. It is a lot more effort on me as a father because when coming home I cannot pursue my own interests. My

children, having no TV, want my attention. It is a sacrifice of love and many times a decision must be made against my own desires. But this is what real fatherhood is about. However, by committing to it our life, our memories, and our future will be richer for it."

When you reason, you realize that the medium really damages you and your family. By getting rid of it, you are freed from its slavery and dictation to you, and the possibility of really being a family begins to emerge. A father relates:

"My wife and I began to go to charity outlets and places which sold goods which were donated to them for their cause and through them I purchased some "National Geographic" magazines and began searching for more. I was able to put together a semi-complete set from 1927 until now. I, in turn, did the same thing with "Reader's Digest." I built a library in our home, now having no TV, and I read to

my children. I have a good reference source to bring to many of life's situations through these and other books while my children are still under my guidance. They really enjoyed this. It is active, not passive like TV, when I'm there but not with them in thought. TV brings me somewhere else and we are all like isolated islands, bunched together, independent of each other, with the waves and winds of TV eroding our shore away, decreasing our size, and making our family more separated. Reading brings us together. It's interrupted sometimes with questions and doesn't always go perfectly, but for the whole, everyone listens and participates."

Life without television will blossom, but only if you fill it with something else: doing chores, participating in hobbies, walking, reading, praying. In fact, it is dangerous to rid yourself of the TV, sweeping your house clean, getting rid of vice and not filling

in the empty space. Being cleansed is not enough
because there is a great desire by evil to dirty what
God has made clean, and in order to bring about
a fall, a host of evil will come upon what has been
cleaned. Filling the emptiness is crucial. Jesus says:

Luke 11:24–26:

> *"When an unclean spirit goes out of a man,*
> *it roams through arid wastes searching for a*
> *resting place; failing to find one, it says 'I will*
> *go back to where I came from.' It then re-*
> *turns, to find the house swept and tidied. Next*
> *it goes out and returns with seven other spirits*
> *far worse than itself who enter in and dwell*
> *there. The result is that the last state of the*
> *man is worse than the first."*

The following letter shows how one family
protected themselves from future attack and filled
in their empty space that the TV left.

Dear Caritas of Birmingham,   10/12/1994

"For the past 15 years, our family has not watched television. This began because of our circumstances living outside the U.S.A. But, living without TV soon became a habit, and then a firm choice. Our seventh child is due in December and we feel thrilled and blessed that our kids know how to spend their time and their God-given talents. We do not mean to brag, so much as to share that it is possible and fruitful to say NO to television. Our kids read incessantly, play musical instruments, sew, bake, create stitchery projects, compose poetry and act. They can problem-solve, take on immense responsibilities, reach out to help others, and defend the truth. We firmly believe they are adept at many "real-life" things, be-cause they are not dependant upon living life vicariously in front of entertainment machines. And — most importantly, they have NOT

been bombarded by the constant materialism, commercialism and erosion of values which is sadly a steady TV diet of America and the world.

"Many of Our Lady's messages have attested to the evils of television and have beckoned us to rediscover the simple, precious value of being together, appreciating each other, and cherishing the presence of Christ in each family member.

"The hardest part is the initial decision. Yes, you will be different. Yes, you will be judged and even ridiculed and, yes, my husband does miss watching sports. But, instead, he's been able to work towards a Master's Degree and has taught himself the beautiful art of stained glass. Yes, there is sacrifice but the resulting gifts, blessings and discoveries are incomparable.

"I like to imagine if all of Catholic America alone would fast from television, what a shock-wave of awareness we could send to the entertainment industry — a potentially profound message: 'We've had enough. We do not need your emptiness and perversion. We dare to be different. We will choose to spend the time in loving one another as Our Lady, Queen of Peace, invites us to!'"

In the Hope,
Love and Promise
of Jesus and Mary,
An American Family in Argentina

A while back, a professor from Russia visited us here in the Community of Caritas and we gathered together for a community dinner. She came in and the kids were playing in their typical way. It was loud and they were being very active. We told her to excuse the noise. She responded:

"Noise! This is life. TV is noise."

A profound statement and her insight about TV was just as interesting. When asked what the greatest threat to Russia was she said:

"Television! TV is a total waste of time, destroying creativity and destroying the youth in Russia. It leads to destruction of respect, honor, and values. It is sadly sweeping through Russia, leading youth into all kinds of fads that lack purpose and wisdom. Yet the youth imitate and follow it. Since TV entered our homes a short time ago, crime has drastically increased, divorce, which was unheard of among those who are Christians, is rapidly increasing, and families are breaking up. We survived Communism but we won't the TV."

Indeed, a great deal has been lost by man in exchange for the deceptive value of television and this is becoming more and more obvious. It's not just "Christian weirdos," as the worldly might tend to say, who think it's demonic or horrible. Feminist author, Adrienne Rich, says:

"Television 'itself' breeds passivity, docility, and flickering concentration." Her perspective is:

"... The television screen has throughout the world replaced oral poetry, old wives tales; children's story-acting, games, and verbal lore; lullabies, playing the sevens; political arguments, the reading of books too difficult for the reader, yet somehow read; tales of 'when I was your age,' told by parents and grandparents to children, linking them to their own past; singing in parts, memorization of poetry; the oral transmitter of skills and remedies; reading aloud; recitation; both community and solitude. People grow up who not only don't know how to read, a late-acquired skill among the world's majority; they don't know how to talk, to tell stories, to sing, to listen and

remember, to argue, to pierce an opponent's
argument, to use metaphors and imagery and
inspired exaggeration in speech; people are
growing up in the slack flicker of a pale light
(TV) which lacks the concentrated burn of
a candle flame or oil wick or the bulb of a
goose-neck desk lamp; a pale, wavering, ob-
long shimmer, emitting incessant noise, which
is to real knowledge or discourse what the
manic or weepy protestations of a drunk are
to responsible speech." [73]

In addition to this, Joyce Nelson, in her book, writes:

"Obviously, making TV programming 'bet-
ter' does not rectify all the losses listed by
Adrienne Rich, each of which has to do with
having the left hemisphere of one's neo-cortex
(brain) effectively amputated by TV, while the
right hemisphere is colonized" (taken over by
the medium). [74]

It is interesting to note that those voices whose ideology one would expect to be most opposed to Our Lady's request to renounce TV are the most in tune, as opposed to Mary's children, who one would think would be most willing to justify its destruction. Many of Mary's children knowingly keep it, not only in the face of Her messages, but also in spite of the brain-damaging effects of TV, along with its capability to have one in or on the brink of sin before one knows it, as well as an unlimited list of other reasons.

The cover of this book, "I See Far," shows the domination the black box has over our being as well as our mind. The illustration shows the eyes completely blocked by video tape, its contents delivered by the medium directly into the mind, thereby completely dominating and confusing (rather fooling) it. It becomes one with the mind demonstrated by the mechanism resembling the brain. The light, which cannot be seen by the individual, shimmers off his face, hands, and scissors. He struggles in torment while he is torn between holding onto darkness (television) which he supports with his right hand or severing the tape. The black box (TV, now a Flat Screen) which keeps him in bondage can be easily removed from his eyes by simply cutting it with the scissors he holds in his left hand. Simply cutting it will allow him to see the light and be free, for his mind to be elevated toward things of God. Sadly the cover speaks the truth, that it is by one hand that we support this vile box, knowing at the same time deep down inside of us that we hold a simple solution in our other hand. The question that confronts and convicts us after reading the truths about this mind dominating slavery is clear. Which decision will you make — the hand severing it or the hand supporting it?

CHAPTER TWENTY

A Revolution To Begin!

It is hoped and prayed that these writings begin the start of a revolt among not only Christians, but all people to throw this medium away, destroy it — not sell it. We invite anyone who wishes to consecrate themselves and their family, and formally accept the invitation of Our Lady, to make the decision to remove this medium from their home and consecrate their families and time to Christ through Our Lady's plans. Ask Our Lady to intercede to Her Son, to correct all errors and take away all the accumulated garbage in you and your family because of this medium, by your formal act of turning away. It is also hoped that hundreds of organizations will spring up to teach and show people these dangers. If you go and tell anyone **"the TV is the voice of satan,"** you

<u>will</u> damage your case. Has your opinion about the TV changed after reading this? If anyone tried to expose to you in one paragraph, in a short conversation, about all the above, a typical response would be, *"He's weird."* Don't make that mistake. Give them this book instead, and pray. To do otherwise will birth a movement against those who are now ready, through Our Lady's invitation, to abandon and reject the medium. You would also become people who, *"you are not to take seriously."* However, presenting all the evidence, such as you have here, proves itself, and truth will prevail in all hearts who are open. It <u>will</u> show them if they want truth. Prudence and a lot of wisdom are necessary not to close the mind of people who are dominated by this medium. The evidence is all there, if they are open to seeking answers. You will not have to worry about persuasion.

The intent of these writings is to light the spark, through Our Lady's messages, to alert people to the anti-message. It won't be done by us or different associations, but through prayer. Then, through collaboration with Our Lady, we will meet success. We must live what Our Lady asks.

When we hire a baby-sitter to watch our children, that's exactly what the baby-sitter does, sits and watches them, takes care of them. It is frightening that what is referred to by the TV, does the same thing as the sitter. It sits there as the TV "set," watching them. Scripture states:

Ezekiel 20: 7

> *"...Throw away, each of you, the detestable things that have held your eyes; do not defile yourselves..."*

Jesus said in Matthew 18: 9

> *"If your eye is your downfall, gouge it out and cast it from you."*

The time of realization has come, a time in which we realize we will not clean up this medium and, even if we could, what would it avail us? We can go on with hundreds of reasons to get rid of something which has done more damage to the spirit of man than any instrument in man's history on earth. It inflamed the L.A. riots.* It was the key element in beginning the war in former Yugoslavia by showing each side, escalating in horror, what the other side did until things erupted in full-fledged war. It was the primary source to spread the idea of plane hijacking. It fosters copycats. Think how many copycats sprang from the idea of one person who put poison in Tylenol, which killed several people. We forget that so many began to do this that the industry, world-wide, had to begin sealing everything from Aspirin to Nestles Chocolate Milk Mix. All because of the spread of a warped idea through the medium.

---

* In March 1991, Rodney King resisted arrest that was captured on a video by a private citizen, who sent it to a television network. For weeks, riots were instigated across the country, inflamed by the media networks.

Television tends to make you think and do what it shows you. Does not the family resemble that which is now seen on soap operas, dramas, and weekly comedy shows? The family has become the copycat and it no longer represents something holy. Our Lady knows that we are led and inspired by what we expose ourselves to and Her plan itself is based on witnessing. Through witnessing and living holy lives, it will spread to others who copy the witnessing and they, in turn, will be copied. To call this copycatting does not seem appropriate, so we say to imitate that witness, or as Our Lady said on June 5, 1986:

> **"Dear children, today I am calling on you to decide whether or not you wish to live the messages which I am giving you. I wish you to be active in living and spreading the messages. Especially, dear children, I wish that you all be the reflection of Jesus, which will enlighten**

**this unfaithful world walking in dark-
ness. I wish all of you to be the light
for everyone and that you give witness
in the light. Dear children, you are
not called to the darkness, but you are
called to the light. Therefore, live the
light with your own life. Thank you for
having responded to my call."**

Jesus is "The Witness." He is "The One"
we should copy and all voices which lead us to do
anything but that, we should avoid. And finally, the
television is viewed as good, like an "angel of light,"
but in his new book, Air Waves from Hell, Father
Frank Poncelet says:

"…THERE WILL BE NO REAL PEACE
IN OUR CHURCH UNTIL THE 'INSTRU-
MENT OF EVIL' IS REMOVED FROM A
SUFFICIENT NUMBER OF CATHOLIC
HOMES — SUFFICIENT NUMBER BY
GOD'S COUNT, NOT OURS. ATTACK,

DESTROY, GET RID OF THAT INSTRU-MENT OF SATAN, 'TELE-VISION.'" [75]

Our Lady is now sent as an angel to give testimony to truth. Finally, in the end of the Book of Revelation, in the epilogue, Chapter 22:12–16, Jesus says:

> *"Remember, I am coming soon! I bring with Me the reward that will be given to each man as his conduct deserves. I am the Alpha and the Omega, the First and the Last, the Beginning and the End! Happy are they who wash their robes so as to have free access to the tree of life and enter the city through its gates! Outside are the dogs and sorcerers, the fornicators and murderers, the idol-worshipers and all who love falsehood. It is I, Jesus, who have sent My angel to give you this testimony about the churches.*

I am the Root and Offspring of David, the Morning Star shining bright."

Just as these writings were completed, the following monthly message was received from Medjugorje. Our Lady said:

October 25, 1994*

"Dear children, I am with you and I rejoice today because the Most High has granted me to be with you and to teach you and to guide you on the path of perfection. Little children, I wish you to be a beautiful bouquet of flowers which I wish to present to God for the day of All Saints. I invite you to open yourselves and to live, taking the saints as an example. Mother Church has chosen them, that they may be an impulse for your daily life. Thank you for having responded to my call."

---

* The newsletter was finished on this date, but was revised and made into a book, March, 1997.

This message is beautiful and to have the gift of being presented to God as a bouquet of flowers is a cause of great joy. But this message is not one of sugar, even though on the surface some may be tempted to view it that way. Television's example offers a path of ease, fun, entertainment and frills; it increases the craving for information. All the saints were examples of persevering in the face of great struggle, loving in the midst of difficulty, enduring prolonged sufferings and hardships, and crying many tears. Their joys were of a divine nature as opposed to those associated with earthly "things" and what they offer.

Turning away from the assumed pleasure of TV may be difficult, but Our Lady's above message is asking for you to be a "<u>saint</u>."

Part Three

The chapters that follow were added in 2020 to update you as to what the medium has now gotten into—many facets of electronics—baby inventions that have grown up to advanced electronics, even more devastating than what its father (TV) was. These chapters are made up of the transcripts of three different *Radio WAVE* Shows by a Friend of Medjugorje—the March 25, 2016, show titled *"Our Lady Doesn't Text, She Calls. Can You Hear Her?,"* the June 13, 2019, show titled *"Are You Really Against Child Abuse?"* and the November 28, 2019, show titled, *"Pied Piper, Babel, Thanksgiving."*

Smart or Stupid?

"Smartphone addiction may have sounded like a punchline at first, but experts caution it is a real and growing problem. In fact, nomophobia, or the fear of being without your mobile devices, is now recognized as a serious enough affliction to warrant checking into a rehab facility!" [76]

CHAPTER TWENTY-ONE

Our Lady Doesn't Text, She Calls. Can You Hear Her?

All Our Lady's messages connect to form a bouquet of how modern man must live to be presented into Eternal Life forever. It is beautiful to see these things unfold and how Our Lady says what She says.

We've spoken many times about the beginning of Our Lady's messages, when She says, **"Dear children..."** This is how She opens Her letter to us, because we read it through words. We don't hear Her voice. We don't have it tape-recorded. So, the first things we see are these words in print. **"Dear children..."** But what follows these words, many times, is the word **"...today..."** Probably 15-20 years ago, I started pointing this out, after the

January 25, 1987, first monthly message, when Our Lady began to say, *"I want you to apply this message **TODAY** in your life. All the mess you have made of your life, all the things in the past, you can't do anything about it. It is water under the bridge. But what you can do is start applying, immediately to your life, the messages to change your future."* You can't change what's happened in the past. But those bad seeds that are producing bad fruit in your life, you now can begin to plant good seeds today, if you act on the messages at this moment. Don't try to fix the past. Start living today so that, as the future comes to you and it goes into the past, you've planted good seeds, and you'll begin picking good fruit.

But what other words are not looked at with seriousness in Our Lady's messages? The ones She says at the end of the message — **"...my call."** It's interesting that She repeatedly and always says this, **"My call."** These are the two words Our Lady's messages always end with. **"My call," "my call,"**

"my call." What does that mean? What does it mean to call? What do you do when you call somebody? What do you use to call somebody? How do you call somebody if you want to? If you need to get in touch with somebody, what do you do? You put out the call. And we use that through the telephone these days, which is now transferred from landlines to cell phones. And so, we make this call to be in communication. Our Lady says to, *"respond to 'my' call."* Where does that take us? What does that mean? Our Lady told us on March 25, 2016:

"…You, little children, are poor in love…"

What does that mean? Our Lady said on March 18, 2016:

"…you must be poor in spirit [to be] filled with love…"

So, Our Lady qualifies on March 25, 2016, **"…You… are poor in love…"** On March 18, 2016, She says, **"…you must be poor in spirit and filled with love…"**

So, what is poor in spirit? I was in Medjugorje for the March 18th apparition. I asked Our Lady, *"Mary, I see this over and over. I see it in the Bible. What does it mean to be poor in spirit? Tell me. Help me to find out. Make it clear to me what poor in spirit means."* Well, I flew out that next day, actually, that night. I'm in the airport, and I have a little prayer book that I carry with me that I never read. I've carried it for two years, thinking, if I ever need it or the plane's going down, maybe I'll open it up and read it. I was sitting in the airport because my flight was delayed for a while. I opened up this little book, which was written by Josemaría Escrivá, who is now a saint. And this is what I opened up to:

"Don't forget it; he has most who needs least. Don't create needs for yourself." [77]

It went on to say:

"Detach yourself from the goods of the world. Love and practice poverty of spirit." [78]

Well, that got my attention. I remembered asking Our Lady, *"I want you to explain to me what You mean by poor in spirit."* It goes on:

> *"...be content with what is sufficient for leading a simple and temperate life."* [79]

Our Lady just said that on March 18, 2016, to be simple. She says:

> **"...you must be poor in spirit and filled with love and mercy. You must have [a] pure and simple [heart] and always be ready to serve..."**

Wow! So, I continued to read this.

> *"What an attachment to the things of the world! But soon they will all slip from your grasp."* [80]

What do you hold every day? What do you do every day? What dictates your day?

Lastly, I read this:

"If riches abound, set not your heart upon them. Strive, rather, to use them generously—and, if necessary, heroically. Be poor in spirit."[81]

These kinds of things are thunder for your life, especially when, a few hours before, you are in Medjugorje and you hear Our Lady say, **"...be poor in spirit..."** I then asked, *"Show me, Mary, every time I see this, even in the Bible. I want to know what this means."*

"If riches abound..." and it does for everybody today, even poor people:

"...set not your heart upon them. Strive, rather, to use them generously, and if necessary, heroically..." [82]

Are you walking through your day, using what you have at hand heroically? Or does it absorb you? Or does it consume you?

Our Lady says today, March 25, 2016, after almost 35 years of apparitions,

"...you still have not comprehended that my Son Jesus, out of love, gave His life to save you and to give you Eternal Life..."

What is it that we don't understand, that we don't comprehend? It is amazing that Our Lady is saying this today. After all our prayers and all that we do, She says, *"You still don't comprehend."* Why is that? Because we're falling further and further from understanding God and Who He is and what He's done for us and the price He has paid. You have to start questioning your life, what are the gods in your life? You have to comprehend that to realize the answer to the question, *"Are these false gods replacing God?"* You would say, *"No. I don't do that."* Are you being honest? Are you properly reflecting and being honest with yourself? Our life is plagued today with idols.

Think about your day today. Reflect on it. How much time did you spend on things that you are absorbed in and you are preoccupied with compared to being absorbed and preoccupied with God? St. Paul says, *"Pray unceasingly."* Our Lady said in a message on April 12, 1987, **"...pray unceasingly..."** It's a repeat exactly of what St. Paul said. You might say, *"Okay. Yeah, I follow the messages. God's always on my mind."* But what, through the day, preoccupied you today or yesterday or will preoccupy you tomorrow? The things that are in our lives, that have our attention, are coming to be our gods, not God the Father. We see families today completely disjointed, completely connected to the world all day long, and not with each other. They can be out eating, and they are all on their cell phones. I read today about some people who were killed in Belgium were talking to somebody on their cell phones at that moment. You might say, *"Oh, that was really good. They were talking to them* *when they got killed.*" No, it's a sign of sickness that, rather than talking to a loved one, they could have been contemplating God.

March 25, 2016

"...you still have not comprehended... my Son..."

And how He died out of love for you. And so, we have broken up family. We have disconnected family. We don't know what it means to follow God anymore. All the Christians will say, *"Yes, we do."* Then why is Our Lady coming, saying this? *"You don't know. You don't understand. You don't know Who God is. You imagine God who you think He is, not how He truly is."* Why does Our Lady say these things? She's trying to reach you, but you're not reflecting because you don't form your day by a Biblical mandate of praying unceasingly and putting yourself in that state where you can.

We have to reflect on what Our Lady's saying when She says:

> **"...I am carrying my love to you. God permitted me to love you...out of love, to call you to conversion..."** March 25, 2016

To call you to conversion means to come to God, to change the direction of your life and see things in a whole different light of the way of God and Who He is and what He expects of us.

So, Our Lady says today, March 25, 2016:

> **"...Therefore pray, little children, pray so that in prayer you may comprehend God's love..."**

How much did you pray today, on Good Friday? You say, *"Oh, I did my four Rosaries."* How much time did you give to prayer if you didn't do that? But what if you did say your four Rosaries? Did that dictate your day, your prayer, or did something else? Were you dealing with other people all day long or with God?

"...so that...you [can] comprehend [His] love..."

You don't reflect, which is a tragedy today. We have a poverty of reflection. We're very poor in the sense that we don't reflect. We don't have time. Our day is structured, completely self-absorbed in things that pertain to us and surround us.

Everything and anything that stops us from reflecting is blocking the ability for us to know God or identify what He's doing. God is actually running after us. He is in pursuit of us, and we're outrunning Him, and He can't catch up with us. Well you say, *"He's God. He can do that if He wants to."* No, He needs your permission. He needs you to stop and start thinking, because you're running toward a cliff that you can't see. And as soon as you make the curve, you're going to fall right off of it. And He's on our heels, but unless we slow down and think, *"He's right behind me,"* this pursuit of His, through His Mother, is after me, I'll never recognize that, and I'll go running off the cliff. Our Lady's words:

> **"...But even today, many of my children do not know Him..."**

But don't think this is just for Muslims or nonbelievers or somebody else. No, this message is to us—dear children. She says many children. You can say, *"Oh, that's not talking about me or this doesn't pertain to me."* It pertains to all of us, because there are aspects in all of us of elements that we do not know God. We do not know Her Son.

> **"...But even today, many of my children do not know Him, they do not want to come to know Him, they are indifferent..."**

What makes you indifferent to God, and what makes you close to God? When you are praying or when you are reflecting or when you are thinking about Him. Every action of your day should be absorbed with God. But again, *"I call you,"* as Our Lady says, **"…my call…"** to review your days, how they're spent, and what kind of things that you're absorbed in. What do you give your time to? What dictates your day? What forms your day?

Our Lady continued on the Second of the Month Message, saying:

> **"…Because of their indifference[s] my heart suffers painfully…"**

Because She can't get a word in. And Her Son, She adds to this painful message after that sentence:

> **"…My Son has always been in the Father…"**

But you won't know that if the things that you do throughout the day makes you indifferent to prayer, and you replace prayer with things of the world.

And so, we have God, in all His effort, chasing us, but we have a free will that keeps us elusive, and we delude ourselves, as Our Lady said, *"You're in delusion,"* because what you think you're doing and the Christian walk you think you're occupied in or that you are a good Christian, you're not at all, or I'm not at all, if I've got a god in my life ahead of Him. What is your god? What are those gods? You've got to start thinking why Our Lady said today, March 25, 2016:

"...you still have not comprehended..."

Do you feel, at the end of the day, indifferent? Have you recognized the miracles that happened today to you? Do you know how many things you might have been saved from or protected from? Or did something happen to you today that you lost protection? You've got to get rid of things that cause indifference, anything that ceases or stops or stymies or takes the place of prayer, causes more indifference to grow. We have a world that's indifferent to God.

In March Second's message, Our Lady said:

"...With Him..."

Talking of Her Son:

"...With Him came the light of the world which penetrates hearts, [and] illuminates them and fills them with love and consolation..."

What blocks that? Why can we not get that?

You need to take time to reflect and make changes in your life. You need to see what makes you indifferent. You need to see what preoccupies you.

What is your day like when you wake up in the morning? What is forming your whole day? What schedules out your day? There's got to be something that is causing us all this indifference, all these things where Our Lady's Son is not recognized, and our actions in living a way of holiness and contemplation. Is the radio always blaring? Are you always on the phone? Are you always texting? Are you always responding? Compare that, add that up in a multiplication, or either, an addition mathematical situation compared to the times that you give to God. What do you give the most time to? Our Lady was not that way. You say, *"Well, She had Jesus."* You can imagine Her life, knowing these things, and then the question that you're asking, compared to the way She lived, and She's told us, *"I did this. This is the way I lived."* She is calling us to do the same thing. You say, *"Well, She didn't have the technology. She didn't have all these things surrounding Her."* You don't have to have that. We here, at Caritas, do not have technology/ electronics in our homes. We don't have cell phones in our homes. We don't have home computers. We don't have home electronics or any games or even electronic toys for our children. Our children are much better for it. They'll grow up, throughout their whole day and their whole life, where God is present every day. He is there. He is not replaced by a computer or a cell phone or electronic toys.

I went to Confession before I left Medjugorje, and the woman next to me in the line had her phone out playing a game. We sat there 20 minutes waiting to go to Confession. She did this right up to the time it was my turn. She was after me and was playing a computer game on her phone the whole time she was waiting in line for Confession. This wasn't a 19 year old. This lady was probably 28 to 34 years old. I don't get it. It's not in my mentality to even understand that. But when you see this happening, you understand why there is no reflection, and therefore, there is indifference.

In the Book of Acts, it talks about a riot of the silversmiths. It says:

"About the time of a serious distur-
bance broke out concerning the way.
There was a silversmith named De-
metrius who made miniature silver
shrines of Artemus [false gods] *provid-*
ed no little work for the craftsman..."

In other words, it made a lot of money for them.

"...He called a meeting of these other
workers in related crafts and said,
'Men, you know well that our prosper-
ity derives from this work...'"

There's a lot of money made on cell phones today,
like little gods, like Artemus. You talk to them. You
call. You use it all day long. It makes you indifferent to prayer, keeps you from prayer, time that you
spent on it today and throughout your months that
you've lived with this thing compared to the time,
each day, you give to prayer. Put that as a verse,
phone versus prayer. See what you're absorbed in.

So, these silversmiths were upset and caused a riot.
It says:

> **"...'Men, you know well our prosper-
> ity derives from this work...'"**

Apple makes a lot of money from this, these
little gods. You think if people threw them away,
they wouldn't get upset? You think if people heard
"My call" and they did what I did...When I started
praying, I was in business. I had the first cell phone.
Probably five hadn't been sold. They were $2,600.
You had to screw the whole thing into your car
dashboard to install it. But, I began to pray shortly
after that, and I had an aversion to it. I knew God
was showing me, _"Get rid of this thing."_ And I did,
because I was listening, but not to that phone. I
had gotten it for business purposes. We run a whole
international mission without cell phones now. You
say, _"I can't do without it."_ That's because you've
fabricated it, making it your life, and it surrounds
you. You say, _"Well, I can't do it because of my_

work." We, at Caritas, do it. And again, as you have read, we are international. How do we do that? We just are not indifferent to God. We connect to Him, and He showed us how to be disconnected from these things and run an international mission. So, the silversmith says:

> "...*'Men, you know well that our prosperity derives from the work. As you can now see and hear, not only Ephesus, but throughout most of the province of Asia, this Paul'...*"

Talking about St. Paul:

> "...*'has persuaded and misled a great number of people by saying that gods made by hands are not gods at all'...*"

"My call"? "Thank you for having '<u>responded</u>' to "<u>my call</u>"? Did Our Lady reach you today or yesterday? Will She tomorrow? And how many texts, how many messages do you respond to throughout the day? Phones? Computers? *versus* **"My call?"** Our Lady? Who has the most time?

Scripture continues, quoting the silversmith, who makes little gods:

> **"...'The danger grows not only that our business will be discredited, but also the temple of the great god Artemis will be of no account, lest she, whom the whole province of Asia and all the world worship will be stripped'..."**

Kind of strange. Well, there was a great riot. They tried to arrest Paul. They wanted to kill him because he was saying to give this up.

Our Lady said something incredible on February 25, 2016:

> **"...You are lost and do not know what your goal is...I am calling you..."**

What does that mean? *"I'm phoning you. I'm send-ing you messages. I'm texting you in a spiritual way."*

"...I am calling you: return to prayer..."

If you return to prayer, what are you going to give up? What are you going to swap out time for?

"...I am calling you...return to prayer with the heart so as to find hope and the meaning of your existence, in prayer..."

She ends that message saying, *"It's my call."*

"...Thank you for having responded to my call."

Are we doing that? No, we're not.

There's a girl by the name of Liz Marks. This is a true story. It tells about what the god in her life was. She was a beautiful girl. Scripture tells us that the wages of sin is death. God does not intend for certain things that do happen to you when you replace Him with something else. And like the silversmiths, all of them made these little bitty gods, and everybody bought them. Now everybody is running around with cell phones. They've got their little gods, and they're nothing…These cell phones are nothing more than a god to you. It's your god in your life. You say, *"Well, Heaven forbids this."* Just walk the streets, you see them everywhere—in every place.

This is what happened to Liz Marks, this beautiful girl whose life was enshrined to her little god. And things happen when you do that which is not God's Will for you.

[LIZ]

I just, I remember sitting at home, thinking to myself, like, "I have no one." My friends were there for me at first, but after a while, they weren't.

[MOM]

I looked up on her Facebook page, and she said on there, "Can anybody please hang out with me today? I don't have any friends."

[LIZ]

Before the car accident, the things I did in high school with my friends were, you know, just go to the high school games and everything. Every weekend, go to a party, go bowling. I was a good student. I was a role model. I was like a popular girl in high school.

[MOM]

My main worry for Liz as a parent before she started driving was the typical teenage things, you know, the drugs and the alcohol and, you know, being safe and hanging around the right kind of kids and keeping her grades up.

I did not think that Liz was connected to her mobile phone. I didn't realize that she loved her phone as much as she did.

[LIZ]

I used my cell phone every second, every minute, every hour. Like, if I didn't have it? I would freak out because I couldn't connect with my friends. I couldn't connect with anyone. I couldn't connect with social media or anything. If I didn't have my cell phone, I felt lonely.

[MOM]

I would ask her all the time, "Liz, do you text and drive?" And she said, "No, mom. I swear I don't. Don't worry. I don't use my phone when I'm behind the wheel."

[LIZ]

I ignored those warnings about texting while driving because everyone else was doing it, so

I thought I was okay. I thought I was invincible. But clearly, I was completely wrong.

[MOM]

I was getting ready for work and then, 12 hours later, I'm in ICU staring at my daughter who's bald and tubes running in and out of her body, and it's just overwhelming devastation over a stupid text.

[LIZ]

The consequences of my life now after the car accident is the fact that I'm blind in one eye now. I cannot smell. I cannot hear very good because a bone broke in half inside my eardrum. I can't create tears because both my tear ducts got damaged, and I can't put my body to sleep naturally. I take medicine to go to sleep.

The hardest part about my life after the car accident was the fact that I was alone. Everyone was away at college. I wasn't. I couldn't drive. I couldn't go to college.

*My friends were there for me at first, but after
a while, they weren't. They got tired of me.
They got tired of all my problems.*

[MOM]

*Don't text your loved ones when you know
they're driving. It can change their lives forever.*

[LIZ]

If you get a text, don't look at it. It's not worth it.

Tragic. Do you know one in four wrecks now,
25% of all wrecks, are caused by this god thing that
we see as so valuable? When you start following the
gods of this world that form your day, that tells you
what you should do throughout the day, that dictate everything you do, there are repercussions for
that, and those repercussions are not just something
physical, like what happened to Liz. It's spiritual.
The void that fills our lives today is being preoccupied and self-absorbed. It's really a selfish thing.

It's selfishness. It's around you. It's your god. It's replacing prayer.

But yet, there are other people that don't make it like Liz did. They die; there are a lot of deaths. Do you want to see your loved ones again? Do you want to have them with you? How tragic it is if you are judged after you die, and you never lived the spiritual life, and you were indifferent to God, that you will lose your life for Eternity.

Our youth are raised here at Caritas to know that God is the very fabric of their life. Our life here, in community, on a daily basis, is 'seamless' between Heaven and earth. Our Lady is all throughout our day, in everything. We are preoccupied with Her messages. There is not a day in my life, or anyone else in the community, that we're not talking about the messages. This is the kind of environment you have to grow into. You have to create it in your family like I did first, and from there, it grows into community. It's the future.

Liz was a beautiful girl. She had friends. She had everything. And when she lost that, she was lonely. She had nobody, because she made her love, through this phone, through her connections, her life. That god failed her. But if she was in prayer, saying a Rosary, would that have happened? How many things that should not have happened, have happened this way? How tragic. How sad.

It's tragic the way we live and what we let form our lives. Many are losing salvation because of it. This little god is the great god of the world today. These phones are out of control, and they now are '**in**' control. People are going to perdition, not so much because of the thing itself, but, because by being self-absorbed, they are indifferent to God. They get on the wrong path. Our Lady said on March 18, 2016:

> "**...I desire to teach you complete trust in God the Father. I desire for you to**

**learn by an internal gaze and internal
listening to follow God's will..."**

How are you going to follow God's Will?
Was it God's Will for this to happen to Liz? What if
she could have learned to have an internal gaze, an
internal listening to **"My call?"** This is what is happening today. There is no trust in God. There is trust
in the false gods. Your whole life is in it. You need
to change your direction now, not later. You've got
to trust completely, surrender to God and believe
Our Lady's words, and She will receive you in your
heart.

**"...You are lost and do not know what
your goal is...I am calling you: return
to prayer with the heart so as to find
hope and the meaning of your existence, in prayer..."**

"Respond to my call." Tomorrow, or even
at this moment, wherever you are, know that God

is calling you. He wants you to be still. To be still means to be quiet. Turn off all the voices when you're in the car tomorrow going to work. And with an internal listening, try to find His Will, and you will, because He's in pursuit of you. Pray with all your heart, with that internal gaze, and you'll feel like the God Who loves you means what He says. You will have an encounter. You seek this, and He'll seek you.

Stop and Pray and Reflect the price of a text.

Stare into the eyes of Liz.

Are you, as a parent, willing to accept the responsibility of consequences by not saying 'no' to your children to have an **idol** that cannot only kill the body, but can also kill the soul?

Stare into the eyes of Liz.

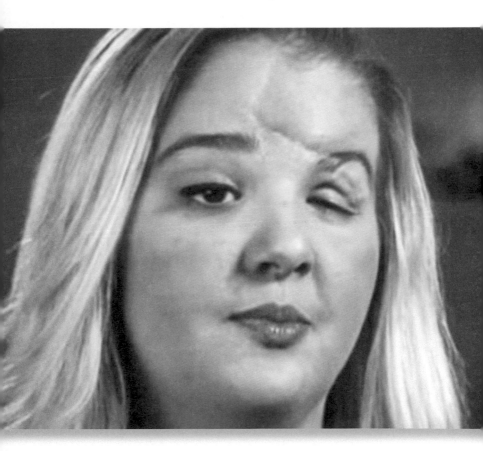

Pray right now. Make a promise to God the Father
and His Son.

Don't risk Eternity.

Make radical changes Now.

Get rid of everything that distances you from God.

The town of Hamelin was once full of rats. The people had grown tired of them, but were unable to do anything. One day, a strange man came to town. He was called the Pied Piper. He was offered a payment if he freed the town of the rats. The Pied Piper started playing his pipe. As he played, all the rats came out and followed him. The Pied Piper walked up to the harbour with millions of rats behind him and led them into the water where they all drowned. When the Pied Piper returned to the town for his payment, the greedy town refused to give him his payment. The Pied Piper then began to play his pipe again. As he played, all the children in the town began to follow him. He led the children away, and they were never to be found again.

Are you allowing your children to never find their childhood?

Will you be guilty of letting them drown?

Are you in the same danger?

CHAPTER TWENTY-TWO

Are You Really Against Child Abuse?

You know that we live in a time like no other. It's why Our Lady has said, through the years, that this is a special time.

June 25, 1993

"...These times are particular..."

Why? Because man has never had, at his fingertips, what we have now. With that, we also have so much abuse on all levels.

The one thing that is disgusting to everybody is child abuse. Almost all people would have an aversion to child abuse, and rightly so. But the question is, have you had a part in child abuse? Are you doing some type of child abuse? Are you allowing some type of child abuse? Are you tolerating some type of child abuse? Many times people don't know what they are doing because they, themselves, are actually doing what is abusive. If you go out on the streets and look around, you see what is happening. Nowhere in history have we lived and done what we are doing now.

Steve Jobs, who died in 2011, was the founder of Apple. What do we know about him? People might say he was a really good businessman. He was a devout Buddhist. He was a pioneer, a vision-ary, if you will, in the technology world. He was a good person, but he was also pretty tough to be around. In 2010, *The New York Times* reported that the mastermind, Steve Jobs, was asked by a reporter how his children love the new iPod. Do you know what he said? *"They haven't used it."* He didn't say they haven't used it yet. He said they haven't *used* it. Was he going to let them use it? Jobs continues, *"We limit how much technology our kids use at home.*" [83] What does that say to you? Are you or your kids unlimited in how much technology they use? Much more, is any technology totally off limits in your home, as Steve Jobs eludes to? Here (Jobs) is the mastermind of these digital devices, and he won't let his own kids use them.

Bill Gates is one of the founders of Microsoft. He made it possible to have a computer in every home. His wife, Melinda Gates, said in an interview in 2017, with *The Washington Post,* in regards to what computers and other technology is doing:

"...adolescents who don't yet have the emotion tools to navigate life's complications and confusions, they can exacerbate the difficulties of growing up..." [84]

And she adds to that:

"...learning how to be kind, coping with feelings of exclusion, taking advantage of freedom while exercising self-control." [85]

What are these people trying to tell us? They are at the top of the electronic food chain, and they are not letting their children do what you are letting your children do, or your grandkids, or other family members. Are you okay with that? They are not!

This technology is a monster and it is very damaging, especially to the youth. Most older people have their habits. Most older people have decided where they're going to go—to Heaven, Purgatory, or hell. Their habits continue into old age and for most, to their death. So satan doesn't spend a lot of time there. Where has satan always been the most active? In the youth. And he's got a prodigy in front of these children that is very, very dangerous, and it's an abuse by the parents. You are committing a very big sin, a very big wrong, that will come back onto you later. You are letting something influence your children, your youth, your adolescents, when you should be doing the influencing.

October 24, 1988

"...your Mother wants to call you to pray for the young of the whole world, for the parents of the whole world so they know how to educate their children and how to lead them in life with good advice..."

The following is about some of the problems with this.

In the article called *"Kids and Digital Dementia,"* it states:

"Research shows that our growing use of digital devices can affect sleep quality, obesity risk, and aggressive behavior. Now there is concern that many young people are suffering from 'digital dementia,' too.

"In South Korea, nearly a decade ago, after doctors began seeing young patients with

brain-function issues that are more commonly found in aging people or those with conditions such as stroke, traumatic brain injury, or tumors.

"Most recent research from around the globe supports this finding: At alarming rates, kids raised in the digital age are developing cognitive problems and attention issues and struggling with memory, organization, reasoning, problem solving, and in-person social communication.

"'Multitasking and rapidly clicking through websites can contribute to short attention spans and impaired learning,' says neuroscientist Manfred Spitzer, MD, PhD, medical director of the Psychiatric Hospital at Germany's University of Ulm. He believes young brains should be allowed to develop with a greater range of use and application than our technology addiction allows.

*"While **digital** dementia can affect anyone, including the elderly, youth might be at a higher risk for overuse of devices because the brain is still developing. Spitzer feels so strongly about the issue that he recommends children avoid media consumption."* [86]

Many would think or say, *"I get it. I can see this is true."* Now that you are armed with the facts, what are you going to do about it? If you respond, "Nothing," then you are a child abuser!

So now you can see clearly, we have problems with digital devices, such as scattered to severe attention deficits, along with many other detrimental damage done to their users. They especially damage the youth, and they open the gate wider for the devil to influence them. A famous talk show on the radio had a caller, a millennial, complaining about other millennials and how off base they are! He said, *"I'm like a fish out of the water."* Talking about fish, in the year 2000, people had the average attention span of 12 seconds. By 2015, it had dropped to eight seconds. So, you go from 12 seconds to eight seconds. Do you know what a goldfish is? What its attention span is? Nine seconds.[87] They can focus longer than those who use these digital devices today. This continual distraction is not a novelty. It is doing something that is hindering at all levels.

I just came back on a plane from Medjugorje recently (March of 2016). Two older women, around 70, sat the whole flight with a screen in front of them, their iPods, which had an 8 × 12 inch screen, playing Solitaire, and other stupid games for hours! I saw one of them putting her finger on the screen, making the ball go up and down. And I'm thinking, what in the world is an old woman doing this for, except satan is occupying their time, mesmerizing these people, so they won't pray, or at least, reflect on their lives.

I was attending English Mass in Medjugorje in May, 2019, and a priest from Cork, Ireland was the main celebrant at Mass. He started his homily this way:

"You cannot pray all of the time everywhere, unless you pray some of the time somewhere."

That parallels St. Paul, in 1 Thessalonians 5:17:

"Pray without ceasing."

That also aligns with Our Lady's messages. She said: May 25, 2013

"...Pray without ceasing..."

That means what it means! You can't pray all the time everywhere, unless you pray some of the time somewhere. We have these two elderly women on the plane, not contributing to anything, except something that is electronic. It's startling. But children are doing the same thing, and at all ages.

In reflection, this was really astounding to me. This is not the first time I've seen this. I can't see what they see in it. I did my four Rosaries. I did Scripture readings. I prayed, and looking at them, I see how lost we are. How can you be 70 years old, headed toward your death some time, and this is what you are being preoccupied with? There's a recent study that was done that showed infants' attention spans suffer when their caregivers' eyes wandered to their smartphones. The caregivers just looking at their smartphones, or other technological distractions, during the play time of children, impairs the capacity of the language acquisition and the children's problem solving! [88]

At Caritas, you can observe the following with children. As adults, you can see in the peripheral vision of your eye, and you know who's next to you or who's praying the Rosary in the Field, etc., because you can see the shirt they have on, that you saw on them 30 minutes ago. Young children do not identify adults in the first couple of years or what the adult is saying without making eye contact. It's a marvelous thing. Every time you see a small child here, they look, not at the blue jeans, but at your eyes. When they're standing up, they look at you to make eye contact. It is a really wondrous thing. They cannot communicate or understand without eye contact. And what was Eve's problem? Eye contact. She couldn't make eye contact with God after following satan's call. So, satan has created something similar to what brought about Eve's fall. And you are allowing the use of these digital devices that are so damaging that they put a lot of youth on the road to perdition.

October 24, 1988

> **"...the situation of the young is difficult. Help them! Help parents who don't know, who give bad advice!"**

"Today, with technology now moving at the speed of light, we are yet to fully understand all of the negative effects to the critical, constructive, and creative thinking capacities of the brain caused by the abuse of technology. **But, we do know this damage is real.**"[89]

CHAPTER TWENTY-THREE

We Are Deceived

Our Lady had to come in 1981, to get rooted before the fax machine became popular, which was around 1987! Our Lady wouldn't be able to get people's attention right now. I am going to tell you now, that if Our Lady appeared today, 2019, to begin Her plans in Medjugorje, She wouldn't be able to do it. There are so many people in Medjugorje with their cell phones. They are so preoccupied and distracted that they couldn't be penetrated. They couldn't be reached.

These digital devices are so dangerous that one recent study showed that the mere presence of a cell phone diminished the quality of conversation. That's a study. I'm not making that up—just the

presence of a cell phone, not even being on it. It
also affects the objective experience of trust to each
other. They lose trust. They lose also empathy, the
closeness between the two people, and having discussions of meaningful topics. They can't penetrate
it. They can't enter into a quality conversation, just
with a cell phone there. [90]

Nicholas Kardaras, PhD, says:

> *"We're social animals and we think technology*
> *is a panacea that's going to keep us connected,*
> *but depression rates are sky rocketing."* [91]

That's another big thing. The youth are in deep
depression. You may see them laugh or have fun or
be in discussions, but they're depressed. And this is
showing up everywhere right now. Kardaras says:

> *"We've been sold this false narrative that*
> *it's connecting us. We've been lulled by how*
> *amazing these devices are, but we didn't fully*
> *vet the dark side."* [92]

These are the professionals in the fields of digital technology. These are people who are looking at these things.

We know that hyper-stimulation is affected by smartphones, and it harms your sleep quality. An article called *"The Health Risks of Tech Addiction,"* says:

> *"Many of us go to bed with our phones beside us making it easy to succumb to the blue glow of the screen until we close our eyes. This blue light disrupts the circadian rhythms, tricking our bodies into thinking it's daytime, which leads to sleep disturbances. Add the temptation to check your phone during the night and you have the ingredients of a poor night's rest."* [93]

And what happens after that with a poor night's rest? Psychotherapist, Nancy Colier, who is quoting this, says:

"We power down our devices so they can reboot, but we need to do the same for ourselves." [94]

We are deceived. And if these devices are doing this to adults, what are they doing to children? I get really physically nauseated when I am out somewhere or at a restaurant and I see someone give a little iPod or a little cell phone to a child, sometimes as young as two years old or three years old. They are immediately silenced. They go into a trance-like state. And they are no problem for mommy and daddy, until they are 15, and they want to end their lives or get on drugs or they go crazy. This is abuse, and one of the greatest widespread abuses taking place.

Again, an important message from Heaven worth repeating.

August 15, 1988

> **"…pray for the young people; talk with them. Young people find themselves now in a very difficult situation…"**

I never do my research; I never write anything
using a computer. All of my writings, all of my books,
throughout all of these years, are all written by pen.
Often, I run the ink right out of the pen in a few days.
All of my books, even the thick ones like, They Fired
the First Shot 2012 and Look What Happened While
You Were Sleeping, were all handwritten. They
Fired the First Shot 2012 was 1000 pages. One typed
page averages out to three handwritten pages, yet, I
don't want to be on a computer. Why? Because it is a
distraction for me. Intuitively, by reason, I know this,
because between me and the writing is a system, attached to a printer. And when the system goes down
or there is some kind of glitch with the computer, I
would have to disengage what I'm thinking about
and try to figure the stupid thing out. I say stupid
because I think they are stupid in a lot of ways, and
I have always had an aversion to them. You say,
"Well, you use them here at Caritas." Yes, we do. But
I don't, and you shouldn't put important and serious

matters on computers. You should have a hard copy of everything that you need to save. Its use in the mission is *"Use it; don't let it use you."* Most everybody is used by these devises. Again, in our community our homes are free of electronics.

I believe and know clearly that these digital devices and technology are going to go away. It's part of what's going to happen. I've always felt that reading a book on the printed page, is God's way to communicate to us. Yes, Caritas has the top, number one Medjugorje website in the world, the most visited around the world, the most comprehensive, the site that the most people stay on of all Medjugorje sites of the world. We do that to bring people into Medjugorje and then to teach them to limit their time on them and then get away from these things. They provide information, but we would recommend that you download and read the information on paper. It will be more meaningful and retainable and, therefore, more comprehendible from the written word.

Anne Mangen, who is a professor at the National Centre for Reading Education and Research at Norway's University of Stavanger says:

"Screens encourage people to skip around rather than digest the text from beginning to end. Scrolling through digital screens consumes more mental resources than turning a page." [95]

I've never read that before. Nobody has ever told me that. But, thoughtful men, being in prayer, fasting, following Our Lady, reading Her messages, they will know that intuitively. I knew this in my heart. I don't need the research from the Norway professor, but Mangen confirms what I believe. Therefore, if you don't accept what I, a ditch digger, says, then you have to accept scientific data. Professor Mangen says that:

"The eye strain caused by screens can be distracting to the brain." [96]

So, you can't engage through the screen like you can enter into a book. There is nothing warmer, more enjoyable, than sitting down with a real book and reading it. Mangen goes on:

"There's a growing body of research that shows we simply pay more attention to words and images on paper." [97]

That's pretty profound. Mangen continues:

"Text on paper has physicality and special extensions that are easily accessible." [98]

With her colleague, Mangen says that the published findings of the *International Journal of Education Research* states:

"When you read a printed book, you can see how long it is and even visualize where certain passages fall. It's like having a map with landmarks to track the narrative." [99]

Astounding, some may say. But why do we need a professional journal of education research to tell us this? It is common sense. I reasoned this out decades ago. I didn't depend on a "group body of research" to know these things. It is common sense! In other words, as I would explain it, reading a hard copy book, you are seeing peripheral in front and behind in what you are reading. You know what's coming. You know where it's going, up and down. You can see the landmarks. You have a narrative. You know where it's going. But those things do not show up on the screen.

Why has it taken this long to discover what I just explained to you? You can come to the same conclusion yourself, as I did. Take responsibility and change what you know is not good for you and, specifically, for your family. Why are these universities and researchers coming up with these thoughts at this stage of the game? You do not have to wait for studies and research. You are perfectly capable of learning the same, simply through prayer and observation.

"Until we get the anhedonia* and digital dementia thing dealt with, we're spitting up a rope wondering why Junior can't pay attention; won't engage in conversation; is sullen and withdrawn; hates himself and everyone around him; escapes into a world of promiscuity, drugs and rock and roll; and, refuses to do anything productive with his life. And all while we pay doctors and therapists to falsely diagnose and dispense medication he too often doesn't need in the first place." [100]

Trace Embry

"Will Our Children be Victims of Digital Dementia?"

---

* "Anhedonia is a destruction of the pleasure center in the brain...It comes mainly from the over stimulation of pleasurable and exciting activities, particularly on many of today's techno-gadgets." [101]

CHAPTER TWENTY-FOUR

The Best Toy a Child Can Have is Another Child*

The American Academy of Pediatrics and Manfred Spitzer, who was quoted earlier in this book, have a **LIST OF SEVEN SUGGESTIONS.** They recommend to, *"Use print media."* This is a different group from Norway, but they came to the same conclusion. They say to:

1. *"Use print media rather than tablets or smartphones for reading to give your child a break from looking at screens."* [102]

The American Academy of Pediatrics is saying this? How come you can't even reason this out? You should already know these things. But see, it is

---

* A Friend of Medjugorje termed this phrase through his constant anthropology of watching what makes children tick and being raised healthy and social.

too appetizing. It is too consoling. It brings a false peace in the house. Everybody becomes silent, but they become unsocial.

> *"...from looking at screens. Studies have shown that reading print materials also boost reading comprehension."* [103]

So, we are not comprehending. Our Lady uses the word comprehension often. On January 25, 1987, Our Lady said:

> **"...You are not able to comprehend how great your role is in God's design..."**

How much less can we now, with all these things that surround us? We are bombarded all day long with digital devices, everywhere.

> 2. *"Practice memorizing things like phone numbers and passwords instead of letting technology track them."* [104]

You ask somebody for their phone number, *"I don't know it. Let me look it up."* It's right in your hand. Most people don't know numbers. They don't have to remember anything. What happens when these devices go away? What's going to happen when GPS goes away? GPS went down on the eastern seaboard in June 2019. The Delta flights were grounded on the whole eastern seaboard because the GPS system was down for about an hour or so. It cost millions and millions of dollars, and how many missed flights were there? We are in such a delicate, thin-ice situation, that when God snaps His fingers, it's gone. Is God going to do that out of meanness? No. He's **'going'** to do it out of love, because it's a false idol. Our Lady said:

August 2, 2005

"...your heart is filled with...false idols..."

What do you think Our Lady meant when She said:

February 2, 2018

"...do not believe lying voices which speak to you about false things, false glitter..."

These little boxes hold voices all day long. Our Lady called them **"false glitter."** It's an idol. So, we know it's going to pass because it replaces God. As you have read, recall the two elderly women on an airplane who didn't have the time to think about God through a nine-hour flight. They played with this stupid thing constantly, instead of just reading a good book or something that can be consoling to your heart or your intellect.

If one does play games, etc., at least do so as the American Academy of Pediatrics suggests:

3. *"Use puzzles and games, such as Chess and Scrabble, that promote real-time problem-solving rather than games that let the computer do the thinking."* [105]

See, you don't have to think today. And because you don't have to think today, when you go to hire these youth, and even adults, they don't know how to think. They were never taught how to think, and it's getting worse.

The next suggestion is:

>   4.   *"Create screen-free zones where no digital technology is allowed—like the dinner table and your child's bedroom."* [106]

How about a better suggestion than that? Just get rid of it. No children should have these things. No teenagers should have it. What about you, as an adult? Does your witness show, and thereby invite them to use the 'things of death?' But see, you've accepted it because you follow the culture, you let it drag you along, with the wave of the tsunami, where we're going. The next suggestion on the list is:

>   5.   *"Ensure your child gets enough outdoor play and physical exercise."* [107]

We don't do that here at Caritas; it just happens automatically. It's natural that our children get exercise. You just create an environment where these devices and technology are not there. The kids have energy. They are made to play with each other. Through my observations here and watching the children, I often have said that, **"the best toy a child can have is another child."** You can't get on the floor for hours. They can. And you know what happens when their batteries run out? They fall asleep. We see them fall asleep on the carpet in the auditorium in our mission building and other places. After their batteries are recharged, they wake back up and they start again. They're regenerated. And they're healthy mentally, physically, and they sleep well at night.

Other recommendations from the list:

6. *"Allow unstructured play time which is critical for learning, problem solving, and skills, and fostering creativity."*

"Develop creativity by offering your child musical instruments, art supplies, physical toys that spark their imagination." [108]

This is almost like kindergarten. Why do we even have to say this? This is so common sense, so simple, so basic. And yet, we have to put out papers from universities to tell parents, *"This is what you need to do."* And the last suggestion on the list is:

7. *"Encourage your child and form them to develop hobbies that aren't related to digital media."* [109]

Our young children in the community play hard all day. They are in a dream environment and are comfortable to fall asleep wherever they are, wherever their batteries run out, in *The Tabernacle of Our Lady's Messages*,* inside or outside.

* *The Tabernacle of Our Lady's Messages* is the Motherhouse building of Caritas of Birmingham's mission.

The community children are around animals all the time in our agrarian "Way of Life." Many times they find playmates in the young animals. After Maddalena and little Pacino wore themselves out playing, they easily shared a bed to take a much needed nap.

Chicken time: The youth need to be around adults throughout the day. Society has built a system where adults and children are separated. First through twelfth grade children are always with the same age group in every classroom, sports, etc. In the above picture, children, youth and adults work together. What about play? This is play for the children, bonding and learning with adults. Much of the millennial generation have no skills—only academics—no apprenticeship. A Friend of Medjugorje always says:

> "In our one-room schoolhouse, academics is second. Apprenticeship is first. Apprenticeship puts academics to use. Skills, trades, carpentry, etc., puts academics to use. Straight academics narrow down abilities, crippling the youth."

Electronic gadgets kill what you see above.

The fast shutter speed makes the kids swinging look slow. But the swing in the hay barn is not only fast, but also exhilarating. Jumping off the 1½ story wall, with two children on the rope swing together, takes skill that does not come with electronics, TV, etc. Many watch life. Our community children live life.

"...don't think the executives in Silicon Valley don't know what they're doing to your kids and mine; because they do. That's why they send their kids to Waldorf Schools.* There isn't a computer to be found in any of the classrooms! Everything is done with pen and paper!" [110]

> *Trace Embry*
> *"Will Our Children be Victims of Digital Dementia?"*

---

* Waldorf Schools strive to develop pupils' intellectual, artistic, and practical skills in an integrated and holistic manner. They do this using no technology through 8th grade and very scarcely in high school.

CHAPTER TWENTY-FIVE

What the Experts and Executives Are Saying

What are the experts and executives and CEOs from Silicone Valley saying? Chris Anderson, CEO of *Robotics and Drone Company, 3D Robotics,* said to *The New York Times*:

> *"My kids accuse me and my wife of being fascist and overly concerned about tech, and they say that none of their friends have the same rules. That's because we have seen the dangers of technology firsthand."* [111]

See, they are also at the top of the food chain. They know what this stuff does. They know what the companies are doing. So, this is what this CEO has done. He sees it. It's amazing what he goes on to say:

*"That's because we have seen the dangers of technology firsthand. I've seen it in myself. I don't want to see what happens to my kids. **On the scale between candy and crack cocaine, <u>it's closer to crack cocaine.</u>"** [112]*

Take that to the bank. He's part of the system and he's confessing.

The former president of Facebook, Sean Parker, speaking at an Axios conference, says:

"The thought process that went into building these applications, Facebook being the first of them...was all about 'How do we consume as much of your time and conscious attention as possible?'" [113]

He ends this quote, saying:

"God only knows what it's doing to our children's brains." [114]

The last statement is a "self-profession" in which there is something happening that is very devastating to our children's brain, but only God knows where this is going to end up, and how deep it is happening. We just know the peripherals of it.

The former executive assistant at Facebook, Athena Chavarria, now current executive assistant of Facebook's Zuckerberg's philanthropy arm, said in 2018, to *The New York Times*:

"I am convinced the devil lives in our phones..."[115]

Did you read what she said? That means possessed! If the devil lives in the phones, then something dark is in these electronics. Keep in mind her position with Facebook.

"I am convinced the devil lives in our phones and is wreaking havoc on our children." [116]

This one quote, and who is saying it, is enough for me, as a parent, to make sure that any youth not have these things, much less one's self. Forget about what their friends have. Let them rebel against it. Don't be in a gray zone. Teach your children, as well as yourself. Decide, tell your children, *"We're not going to have it. It's not part of our life."* They will respond, *"Well, all my friends have it."* Your response, *"Well, they do, they can do what they want."* By being a witness and mandating they will not have these devises, you're not putting them in the gray zone. You're showing them black and white. You show them, *"Don't cross this line. We're not going to do that."* They may not like it. But for you, who have young children, don't ever let them get on it again. You, yourself, need to be the witness.

Tim Cook is the current CEO of Apple. The big Apple. Do research on Apple and how it got its name and where it came from back in the '50s. Who was the first guy to crack the ability to create a computer. Look what happened to him. He was of an abominable lifestyle. He poisoned an apple, and took a bite out of it to end his life. You may question this and do a fact check on all of this and say, *"Oh! well, Steve Jobs didn't name his computer 'Apple' because of that man who cracked open the secret to make the computer. Jobs named it Apple because he's around apple orchards and all these kinds of stories. Or it was some of his partners that came up with the name."* Well, that's true in the physical world. But the physical world is driven and is led by the spiritual world. So, if you look at the spiritual world, you'll find exactly what I'm saying. And that's how you see the fingerprint of satan. And do you know how much Steve Jobs' first Apple Computer sold for? It sold for $666.66! Whoa, whoa, whoa, whoa! You mean 666 of Revelation? Remember, it has the bite of the apple of Eve on it. And this man, who cracked the secrets to create computers, poisoned an apple, and took a bite out of it and was found dead. So how does Jobs' computer end up with the trademark of 'one bite' out of the apple and named Apple? He had to know the origin of that! And if he didn't know the origin of it, satan inspired it. The spiritual world inspires the physical world—both the Light and the dark, who are continually at battle against each other.

So, now that you've heard the price, and if you do have any doubts that this comes back from the abominable, the apple, instead of what a fact check may tell you, oh, it's just from Jobs and his buddies, how do you end up $666? There's no chance! Our Lady said:

September 2, 2016

"...Nothing is by chance..."

And then the emphasized "dot" the cents, .66. So we have $666.66, "66" cents emphasizes who is behind it. There's no way that the spiritual realm didn't guide these names and the price and many other things in the computer world.

satan leaves his fingerprint; Our Lady leaves Her Fingerprint. We're in an epic situation. Go research the story. It is unbelievable, and at the same time, fascinating and revealing, remembering you read what Mark Zuckerberg's executive assistant, Athena Chavarria said:

"I'm convinced that the devil lives in our phones and is wreaking havoc on our children." [117]

These false god idols are not for a good purpose. It's for a damning purpose, to send many people to perdition.

Need more proof? Apple CEO, Tim Cook, was quoted in *The Guardian* in 2018:

"I don't have a kid, but I have a nephew that I put some boundaries on. There are some things that I won't allow. I don't want them on social networks." [118]

He didn't say some of them. He didn't say limit the time. He said, *"I don't want them on social networks."* Think about that. Contemplate these things. I didn't learn all of this from these quotes. I knew it through the messages and through prayer and through fasting and have an aversion to these things. I have a clear aversion to these things. They are horrible. I'm speaking about the smartphones and cell phones, etc., and how they are used.

The former Apple senior vice president, Tony Fadell, who was one of the major developers of the iPod and the iPhones, said on Twitter:

> *"Apple watches Google phones, Facebook, Twitter. They've gotten so good at getting us to go for another click, another dopamine hit, they now have a responsibility and need to start helping us to track and manage our **digital addiction across all usages**."* [119]

He also said in a 2018 *WIRED* commentary:

"When it comes to digital nourishments, we don't know what a vegetable or a protein or a fat is." [120]

In other words, we read these things on the cans of food. It tells you what everything is. This is protein, this is fat. He's saying, as far as digital, nobody's putting a label on technological devices. Fadell says:

"What is overweight? What is underweight? What does a healthy, moderate, digital life look like?" [121]

He's making an incredible point. He continues:

"I think that manufacturers and app developers need to take on this responsibility before the government regulators decide to step in."[122]

That's what all this research is coming to. They're going to have to label these things because it's dangerous for your health, your mental health, your depression, your life, your happiness, everything. Fadell continues, saying something amazing:

> *"Decide to step in as with nutritional labeling. Interestingly,"* he says, *"we already have digital detox clinics in the United States. I have friends who have sent their children to them. But we need basic tools to help us before it comes to that."* [123]

Reddit's co-founder, Alexis Ohanian, stated on *CNBC's Squawk Box*, in 2018:

> *"My wife and I both want our daughter to be bored."* [124]

Why would a high profile tech say that? Our kids here at Caritas are never bored because we let them be bored. We don't give them much at all. They're out there playing with the dirt. They create things. When they get bored, they learn, and then they start being creative. Ohanian continues:

"My wife and I both want her to know what it's like to have limits on technology. So we'll be regulating her screen time pretty heavily."[125]

So, the quote is a little bit vague, but what they mean through boredom, they're going to find something to do instead of just being bored. And that's healthy.

Facebook senior executive, Chamath Palihapitiya, says something profound.

"There is no screen time whatsoever for my children." [126]

Chamath is not even giving his children the opportunity to see a screen. Does that not speak to you for all your nieces, your grandchildren, your own children, your adult children? Does this speak to you?

Appropriately, a last quote concerning that we are the last generation who knows two different worlds. Former Google product manager and former Facebook engineer leader, Justin Rosenstein says:

> *"It is very common for humans to develop things with the best of intentions and for them to have unintended negative consequences."* [127]

In other words, anytime you create something, there are positives for it, but there are always negative consequences. Rosenstein goes on and says something else, a very important observation.

> *"One reason I think it is particularly important for us to talk about this, now, is that we may be **the last generation that can remember life before what we have now**."* [128]

That's profound. Do you realize what he's saying? We have people so grown up with this now, that there's going to be people asking, *"Hey, what was it like, what was it like before the airplane?"* Those who lived before man could fly, witnessed the beginning of man's first flight. I remember asking elderly people, in the 1960s, what was life like before airplanes. They told me about it and also what they did when they saw the first airplane fly over. They said, *"We ran outside and ran after it across the field until it flew out of sight. We then fell down, laughing, so thrilled we were."* We now have the last vestige of people on the earth that knew life before the technology took over and enslaved the world.

But thank God Our Lady is here. What is She here for? Because She's going to bring us back from these things. This is all secular stuff, all the reports, everything they're talking about, that this is a bad thing. It's not good. And it's not leading to a good path. And it's amazing that it's the highest people in the industry saying these things. Oh yes, some of them are completely in love with it, but if they're honest they wouldn't be.

So, we have this situation with Our Lady. She says September 2, 2010, what we need to do, and about what this time is. What is it? She says:

> **"Dear children, I am beside you because I desire to help you to overcome trials…"**

What is the trial? Being associated, embracing, accepting, and tolerating these evil things, we need to realize that everything is falling apart, everything is passing, only the glory of God remains. So, we've got evidence, secularly, these things aren't glorifying God. Our Lady has never spoken about technology and its use. Our Lady speaks in agrarian terms, such as nature, seeds, harvest, and waves in the ocean. She's speaking all about nature, which is something so prevalent in our daily life. She doesn't even mention technology. That's a statement right there. I'm here, She says:

> **"…I desire to help you to overcome trials, which this time of purification puts before you…"**

We are going and will go and will continue to go into purification of all that is not of God.

So many of these things come under what Cardinal Alfonso Trujillo, former head of the Pontifical Council for the Family, told me, while I was at the Vatican, *"Many good people are doing bad things."* It's not that you're bad, or it's not that you're doing wicked things, but we're doing some bad, bad things—bad decisions due to satan's strong influence in today's society. And a lot of it is based in selfishness because it takes more effort to live without technology. And sometimes it's necessary to draw the line in the sand that we don't cross over. We have to come into a new life. Our Lady's calling us to it. And She's made it very clear that if you don't begin this now, in the "Time of Grace," you will deeply regret it and have great difficulties in changing over to where you have to live and that you didn't choose to live this way in the "Time of Grace," that you could have done it.

Advance yourself into the future through the messages now. There are hundreds of readings and audios from Caritas that can help you see and understand so many dangers that surround us on a daily basis. Even if you have read them or listened to them before. Read them again and they will speak to you. It is the most important material for you to help you better meet the future. Without reading and listening, you will not be ready for what is coming.

A Fairy Tale Becomes a True Tale

You, with your masquerading, and you always contem-
plating what to do in case Heaven has found you. Can't
you see that it's all around you? So follow me.

Hey, come on. Follow me. I'm the Pied Piper. Follow me.
I'm the Pied Piper, and I'll show you where it's at. Come
on. Can't you see? I'm the Pied Piper. Trust in me. I'm the
Pied Piper, and I'll show you where it's at.

Girl, don't be scared to move. What are you tryin' to
prove? It ain't true that your life has kicked you. It's your
mind, and that's all that's trickin' you, so step in line.

Hey, come on. Follow me. I'm the Pied Piper. Follow me.
I'm the Pied Piper, and I'll show you where it's at. Come
on. Can't you see? I'm the Pied Piper. Trust in me. I'm the
Pied Piper, and I'll show you where it's at.

Come on. Follow me. I'm the Pied Piper. Follow me. I'm
the Pied Piper, and I'll show you where it's at. Come on.
Can't you see? I'm the Pied Piper. Trust in me. I'm the
Pied Piper, and I'll show you where it's at.

Come on. Follow me. Come on. Trust in me. Come on.
Can't you see? Come on. Follow me. I'm the Pied Piper.

CHAPTER TWENTY-SIX

ELECTDEMONICS
Who Do You Follow?

It is an amazing thing to see how people follow each other into the water to drown. I'm dumbfounded when I talk to people in the electronic side of everything, and they all agree with me that everybody's doing this. People go to restaurants. They don't talk to each other. They're following something that has captivated them, tantalized them. Our Lady said, as you have read:

February 2, 2018

> **"...My children, do not believe lying voices which speak to you about false things, false glitter..."**

On August 2, 2005, which was 15 years ago, Our Lady said:

> **"...I have come to you with open arms, to take you all into my embrace, under my mantle. I cannot do this..."**

What? The Virgin Mary with all the power of God behind Her? God has commissioned Her to come to the earth, and She is telling us about something She cannot do? How is that possible? She's the Queen of Peace. She has all the might of Heaven.

> **"...I cannot do this while your heart is filled with false glitters and false idols..."**

What do you think She's talking about? To do this, She continues:

> **"...Cleanse your heart..."**

How do you cleanse your heart? You've got to get away from what makes your heart dirty or from cluttered or glittering, false idols. Now, you tell me what this message is about, because you ignore this over and over and over again. What is the idol? What is the glitter?

"...Cleanse your heart and allow my angels to begin to sing in it!..."

What is singing in your heart? Babel, total babel. Our Lady is here for the destruction of the Tower of Babel. It is coming. Why are you staying connected to it? We don't need this thing. We have proven that. Caritas of Birmingham is the largest Medjugorje center in the world. It is an international mission, seven hours difference in timing, with people working across the ocean and on this side of the ocean at the same time. We output things to the whole world. We send materials to 197 out of 211 countries. We have our presses running full time. We put things out constantly. All without cell phones! The culture thinks social media makes people closer.

"Oh, this lets us share things with each other."
As it is important to revisit this point, these devises
give the appearance of being social, however, they
are not. They are anti-social. They separates us,
because when we separate each other, we separate
ourselves from God, because this electronic system
makes our hearts cold and our neighbor's heart
cold, and we're not really close anymore. We have
let something come between us. It's not theoreti-
cal. All you have to do is go to any restaurant, any
place, stand on the street corner, you will see isola-
tion—introverted people, talking to what they think
is being social. Social media is social? It's anti-social! Anti-God!

I was in an apparition of Medjugorje visionary
Ivanka's, on June 25, 1989. satan has special plans. This
is 1989. What's happened since that time? Our Lady
said:

**"...you are in great temptation and
danger because the world and material**

goods lead you into slavery. satan is active in this plan...”

We already know, in the messages, that Our Lady has condemned consumerism and modernism. Identify these things in your life.

So, I tell you, very strongly, that the Tower of Babel has been built, and if God doesn't come down with Divine Intervention, we are doomed and we are over, because almost no one is going to throw all these things away today. It has to be taken from them. And if it's going to be taken from you, why are you not getting your life straightened now, so that you can live without it? Your answer is: *"I don't think I can live without it."* Can you? No, you can't, because if you understood it, and if you believed these words, and if you believed what Our Lady says about glitter and what captivates you, you would throw this thing in the garbage. Yes, I know that I'm speaking stronger than ever about these things. And you give them to your children. Just hold the hands of your kids and lead them to the devil and say, *"Here. I'm giving the whole hearts of my children to you, Mr. Pied Piper."* Is this being too severe? No. I'm warning you. Our Lady has said those words.

December 2, 2007

> **"...Today, while I am looking at your hearts, my heart is filled with pain and shudder..."**

That's scary. The Mother of God looks into our hearts, Her little children, who are following the Pied Piper.

> **"...My children, stop for a moment..."**

Stop following the Pied Piper. he's leading you to the water to drown you!

> **"...and look into your hearts..."**

She says:

> **"...Is my Son, your God, truly in the first place?..."**

I'm asking you that question because Our Lady asks you that question. Are your children's hearts filled with God first, truly, or they are filled with "electdemonics"? Cast those electdemonics away. Exorcise them away from your children. Our Lady continues:

> **"...Are His Commandments truly the measure of your life?..."**

Be truthful with yourself. Analyze these things. Look at it. And then Our Lady says this very special sentence:

> **"...I am warning you again..."**

When the Mother of God comes from Heaven and says, I'm warning you, you better take that to the bank. She continues:

> **"...without faith, there is no God's nearness. God's Word..."**

That's pretty incredible. God's Word, satan wants to mock the Word. That's why we call it Babel, and that's what we have going through the day, all day long, constantly, people sleeping with their cell phones.

"...God's Word, which is the light of salvation..."

That's where you get your salvation from. His Word, not the Babel.

"...and the light of common sense..."

It's just very simple. It's not filled with complexities.

We're like rats. The whole world is full of rats. And the Pied Piper is bringing us there. But more dangerously, we adults, we rats, are letting the Pied Piper pipe his tune to little children, 8 years old, 10 years old, 15 years old, 16, seventeen, 18. Those are little children as much as you are. I'm telling you, you're not a good parent if you're letting your children do this. Reread Our Lady's messages. Listen to Her Words. I am not saying anything here that Our Lady has not said.

We recognize we're sinners, but one thing we won't do, we will not ignore Our Lady. We see this clearly, and the more we pray, the more we see it, the more we understand it's our undoing.

The purpose of fables and stories is virtue. The Pied Piper speaks truth because the rats are the adults today that satan is leading away into the water to be drowned, and the whole system and everybody with it will drown, because we are replacing God with the god of technology. And what happens from there? What happens with the children? That's what the Pied Piper did. He brought the children after the rats. And that's where we are. It's a very dangerous situation, and it's real. It's not a fable.

Hey, come on. Follow me. I'm the Pied Piper. Follow me. I'm the Pied Piper, and I'll show you where it's at. Come on. Can't you see? I'm the Pied Piper. Trust in me. I'm the Pied Piper, and I'll show you where it's at.

Who will you follow? It is your choice.

Lingering Questions, Comments, And The Answers

Dear Caritas,   *May 6, 1995*

"Although we agree with you on network television being mostly satanic, we feel that the Virgin Mary would not condemn television completely. There are so many great programs and videos that can be seen on television, ie: EWTN, The Trinity Network, and videos like <u>The Miracle of Fatima</u>*,* <u>The Song of Bernadette</u>*, etc. We are able to say the Rosary with wonderful Priests, sitting in front of our TV. The Catholic Mass is also available on at least two channels daily more than once a day.*

"People who throw their TV's out, are throwing the baby out with the bath water. They need a little self control. All sets have on/off

buttons and they don't have to watch the trash programs. I am sure that Mother Angelica of EWTN would not suggest people throw out their sets. She probably would suggest a little personal discipline."

Sincerely,
Pulaski, Tennessee

Dear Pulaski,

*"Thank you for your letter. We do appreciate your concerns and see your sincerity in what you wrote. In response, we do not edit Our Lady's words. What Our Lady says, we fully believe. She said to **'avoid television.'** It is obvious Our Lady meant television as a complete whole because Her next words validate that She meant good programming by singling out the bad as separate. Her words go on to say **'particularly evil programs.'** This message breaks down TV — those programs*

*which are not evil and those which are evil. It is clear Our Lady is speaking of both, putting particular emphasis on evil programs. Her words **'avoid television, particularly evil programs'** speak clearly that both sides of the spectrum are to be avoided. We have seen tremendous fruit in families who have followed Our Lady's words without compromise, and they are the greatest testimonies as to the truth we printed. We know many use TV with good intentions, and we condemn no one who does. We, ourselves, also did the same in promoting Medjugorje until Our Lady slowly revealed, through Her messages and the Holy Spirit, where She was leading us here in the Caritas Community.*

"You wrote that you are in agreement that TV is mostly satanic and also question the throwing away of the TV set as equaling to the baby/bath water analogy. It is important

*to note that satan always packages things this
way, presenting some good, which he hates, in
order to be successful in bringing much bad,
which to be successful, he knows he must do.
So people who bring in cable for these good
intentions also bring in the sewer of many
other programs and channels. Overall letters
to us reveal that the on and off buttons are not
always used. Human weakness prevails and
children, as well as adults, view things they
never should, not to mention the wasted time
better spent in prayer, works of charity, reading, or being with family.*

*"In response to Mass and prayers on TV,
one person wrote to us of a friend who has
become a couch Christian, praying with the
TV and even believing that by viewing Mass,
they are attending it. We do not know of any
theological judgements made that say you can
attend Mass through the TV, and we find it*

difficult to believe, with the messages of Our
Lady of Medjugorje, that She would bless
these actions. She pushes and nudges us con-
stantly to make the effort, go to Mass, pray, etc.
such as the following:

> **'Thanks to all of you who have come**
> **here** *(to Church)***, so numerous during**
> **this year, in spite of snow, ice and bad**
> **weather, to pray to Jesus. Continue,**
> **hold on in your suffering. You know**
> **well that when a friend asks you for**
> **something, you give it to him. It is**
> **thus with Jesus. When you pray with-**
> **out ceasing, and you come in spite**
> **of your tiredness, He will give you**
> **all that you ask from Him. For that,**
> **pray.'** *(December 1, 1983)*

The next day Our Lady said, regarding the
cold:

'Be kind to come to Mass without looking for an excuse. Show me that you have a generous heart.' *(December 2, 1983)*

Again on February 15, 1984:

'...When it is cold, you come to church; you want to offer everything to God. I am, then, with you...'

And more confirmation that Our Lady wishes for us to go to a Church and attend Mass rather than watching it:

'My children, I wish that the Holy Mass be for you the gift of the day. Attend it, wish for it to begin. Jesus gives Himself to you during the Mass. Thus, look forward to that moment when you are cleansed. Pray very much so that the Holy Spirit will renew your parish. If people attend

Mass with lukewarmness, they will
return to their homes cold, and with
an empty heart.' (March 30, 1984)

"These are but a few of many messages that
have taught us what Our Lady desires. We
have also seen wheelchair victims go to church
for Holy Mass, some who are daily communi-
cants, so an excuse about Mass-watching for
most disabled can be overcome with any who
will to do so and attend. In the end, time spent
watching Mass can be spent, with a little more
effort, actually attending it. Our book on TV
was through a very broad perspective which
came through Our Lady's messages, of which
we arrived through years of prayer. It is where
Our Lady has led us.

"It is important to note the Israelites insisted
on divorce. Jesus said their stubbornness is
why Moses allowed divorce, which in the law
of the chosen was accepted. Jesus upheld what

truly God wanted and said no more divorce.
Our Lady does the same in regard to TV. In
our stubbornness, we at Caritas used TV in the
beginning, falsely believing that it was so valu-
able in the rebirth of the Church when, in fact,
the birth of the Church had not this media
and yet grew with the most difficult of circum-
stances. We simply don't need it to spread Our
Lady's plans and Christianity any more than
the early Christians needed it.

"We cannot speak for anyone else in regard
to what they might suggest, but when it comes
to suggestions, we will go with the Queen
of Peace, and She suggests and invites us to
***avoid it.** We found that difficult to do with it*
sitting in our homes, and it eventually led us
to throw it out. We found peace, freedom, and
joy in doing so, and we encourage and invite
others to do the same, but condemn no one
who chooses not to.

"We hope this may give you a little more perspective, and we suggest to reread I See Far. It is of a nature and depth of which must be read several times with deep prayer."

A Friend of Medjugorje

* * * * * * * * * * * *

Dear Friend of Medjugorje,

"What about the news?"

Pensacola, Florida

The following was sent recently by a pilot. It proves that you don't get the truth, not only from the news, but even the weather.

*"The following is a conversation between myself, a pilot, and the Gainesville, Florida flight service station on July 11, 1996, the same day that Hurricane **Bertha** was predicted to hit the coast of Florida. The TV weather reports were painting a grim picture for Jacksonville by late*

*that afternoon. It was blared across the TV
screens on all the channels. Interstate 95 was
already jammed by people who were evacuating. The text was as follows:*

GFS: *Gainesville Flight Service*

P: *Pilot*

GFS: *Good Morning.*

P: *Hi. N2285S is at Craig, and I want to leave
later this afternoon northwest toward Columbus, Georgia and was wondering what time I
could get out.*

GFS: *Whenever you want.*

P: *What about Bertha? I heard it was moving to
the coast of Jacksonville by tonight sometime.*

GFS: *Who said that?*

P: *The TV shows it moving toward the coast, and
people are evacuating several areas. The army*

guard at Craig has put all the choppers in hangars, and the FBO is taking my plane off tie-down and putting it in a hangar.

GFS: *Well, I don't know what radar they are looking at, but I show Bertha two hundred miles east of Bermuda and not doing anything. She has sustained winds of one hundred three but is only moving at thirteen knots per hour. As a matter of fact, it was on a heading of three hundred ten degrees but has now turned to three hundred twenty-five degrees. The Carolinas may have a problem in a day or so.*

P: *So nothing tonight?*

GFS: *From what I can see, you can go have a nice dinner, take in a movie, and then leave.*

P: *OK, thanks.*

GFS: *Talk to you later.*

"I left that same night after sunset. At the time of departure, skies were clear and winds calm. Being a pilot, I have seen this more than once. With weather radar now accessible to virtually everyone, even to their homes, how is it that big TV stations can be so inaccurate in forecasting, which routinely goes way beyond in reference to time (hours in this case) in regard to radical changes in weather? I have only one conclusion — money and ratings. They thrive by people tuning in, and ratings bring more advertising dollars. Stores are hit in the panic buying, and the circle perpetuates itself. Add to that the moral decline as a result, and the next situation becomes more distorted, more exaggerated. Those nice smiles on TV are deceptive, to say it nicely."

* * * * * * * * * * * *

When Medjugorje visionary, Marija, came to America in 1988 and spent two and a half months near Birmingham, Alabama, she had daily apparitions from Our Lady. Many significant things happened and many messages were given. Two things were significant which shed some light — not the words of Our Lady, but Her actions. When Our Lady appeared in the Field on November 24, 1988, before the apparition began, Marija said to pray and not take pictures. During the apparition, a TV team moved right into the middle of everyone near Marija. Our Lady gave Marija an important message for everyone, blessed everyone, and quickly left. There was joy over what Our Lady said and did but disappointment that She left so abruptly. We understood it was because of the intrusion of the camera, and from that point on, there was particular effort to ban TV crews from the Field.

As Marija's visit drew to a close, television stations exerted so much pressure that they were

granted permission to set up their cameras
early in the afternoon in the bedroom where
Marija received Our Lady's apparitions and
messages. Marija was out buying a few things
in preparation for her return to Europe two
days later. Everyone waited, and Marija was
late. When she arrived, she said Our Lady
had already appeared to her. She, herself, in-
dicated she did not know why Our Lady went
ahead and appeared rather than wait a few
more minutes until she returned. Meanwhile,
thousands had gathered and were waiting
for Marija. Marija told them Our Lady still
blessed them and prayed over them all. When
Marija walked past the bedroom, she saw the
cameras. She then nodded towards the bed-
room and said, "That is why Our Lady didn't
wait, She doesn't care for that." Quickly, we
realized it was a mistake to have allowed the

*television station to come in; and this was a
strong lesson.*

* * * * * * * * * * *

5/9/95

*Dear Friends of Our Mother Mary
and Her Son Jesus,*

*"I am Bro. Tony Droll, originally from the
small town of Carey, Ohio. I had the privilege
of coming to Zambia as a missionary early in
1965 and have since been involved in teaching,
social ministry, refugee relief ministry and for
the past 11 years in pre-novitiate formation of
young men who wish to become Franciscan.*

*"For quite some time now I have been privi-
leged to be receiving your Caritas Newsletter,*
which I prayerfully read and pass on to others.
I have found the words written in the newslet-*

---

*   I See Far_{TM} originally was published in newsletter form.

ters to be, without a doubt, inspired and the fruit of hours of prayer. It is therefore one of my objectives to let you know that I not only receive the newsletter and read it prayerfully, but I deeply appreciate the fact that you send it. I work to spread the inspired writings of the newsletters.

*"I recently read **I See Far**. I read it prayerfully over a period of a couple of weeks. I can powerfully relate to what you have to share. The scourge of television has been in Zambia for most of the 31 years that I have been here. It is small yet, with poor equipment. Even today, the single channel begins its programs at 5 PM and ends shortly before midnight. It has news, agricultural programs, household programs and a number of interviewing programs, local plays, time for the president to address the people etc. More recently they began to bring*

in some of America's trash such as Dallas,
Dynasty, The Bold and Beautiful, etc., which
have absolutely no value whatsoever except to
show the corruption in the lives of people. It
is now moving toward films with violence and
sexuality. For many years, President Kaunda
banned absolutely any kissing scene on the TV
(even mother kissing her son) and even that
has changed. I can honestly say that I see the
change in the lives and attitudes of our beauti-
ful Zambian people when TV comes into their
lives, especially with the children.

"St. Joseph's Mission, where I live at our
Formation House, is in the rural area. In fact
my entire ministry has been in the rural area,
beginning with the very deep West of Zambia,
350 miles from a tar road or railway. In all
my time here, I have never ceased to be fasci-
nated with the way the African child lives and
plays. I can attempt to explain it but only to

see it is to experience it. They have NO toys or gadgets to play with and yet there seems to be no end to their brilliance in inventing new games. They play soccer from an earliest age with two stones for a goal and plastic bags wrapped tightly in a ball and tied with strips of old rubber from worn out bicycle tubes for their ball. They have running games and tagging games and every sort which stretches the imagination of the spoiled Westerner. They enjoy themselves so much that they shriek with laughter and joy. In fact they can be so noisy playing, with natural delight, just outside my room window that I often have to close the window in order to concentrate on my writing or reading. Why are they so natural and delightful? I believe it is because they have not been spoiled by the Western world and media.

"I come back to the USA for a home leave every three years (I would love to stop by

*Caritas sometime for a visit) and honestly
enjoy sharing with my family and friends.
One thing I do not look forward to, though, in
the USA, and I do not find to be a joy, are the
American children. I am constantly shocked
by the way they sass and answer back to their
parents, always demanding. They have absolutely everything at their disposal and yet
demand more. They have 50 times more junk
and toys than they need, and want more. They
use whining techniques to get what they want,
and unfortunately, all too often, they get it,
which encourages them to use the same means
again. They eat so much junk food and sweets
that many of them are already out of shape
before their teens. In comparison to how I see
a good percentage of the American children,
our little African children are 'angels.' They
are pure delight to be around. Unspoiled.
Creative. Bright. Intelligent. High spirited.*

They can come to Mass, which can easily last 2 to 2½ hours or more and they do not make noise or draw attention to themselves or make demands. If in any way you can relate to my view of American children, you would go absolutely flips over our children here, beginning with the big eyed, curly headed babies who ride on their mother's back unless they are sucking her breasts and who rarely cry. Surely it must be all of the security from the natural contact with their mother's body that begin them on the path of being the delightful, undemanding little beings that they are.

"I must watch myself; I could write on and on about the natural beauty and spontaneity of our children. And I would credit very much of this purity to the fact that they have <u>no TV</u>; compared to our American children who are literal 'slaves' of the TV. Last year in August I had the rare privilege of going into

the very center of the Kalahari Desert with my Provincial, and good friend, from America.

I am sending a photocopy of the article as it appeared in the local newspaper of my little hometown in Ohio. Take notice of what I have highlighted about the children. I think I have found one of the last places in the world where the purity of the children is of such beauty that it even surpasses that of our local children. Why? The answer, as it appears to me, is in the last paragraph where I am saying much the same as you wrote but considerably more brief and in different words.

"In conclusion, let me assure you that I fully support you and your ministry of bringing the Good News of Jesus through His Mother to as many people as possible. On my part I will continue to promote the same message here in Zambia as much as I am able."

Bro. Tony Droll

The following is the newspaper article that Brother Tony mentioned in his letter. It appeared in his local hometown paper in Ohio and it is about his experiences during his visit to the very center of the Kalahari Desert.

Brother Tony visits country "where the Lord dwells."

I recently had the privilege of making a journey deep into the Kalahari Desert, a trip which an American friend (priest) and I planned nine or 10 years ago and only now were able to realize. It became more than a trip or a break from the daily grind of training young Zambians to become brothers and priests; it became a pilgrimage to where the Lord dwells. It was a prayer; a meeting with God, where there are few signs of life and fewer distractions to divert one from His presence.

The desert can be aptly explained by quoting the back of a postcard we found in Botswana,

"The Kalahari, the largest unbroken mantel of sand in the world is one of the least traveled regions on earth. It has its heart in Botswana but spills over into neighboring countries. Kalahari! The name brings to mind thoughts of unending thirst; land with white-thorned acacia shrubs silhouetted against a blood red sunset; of hunter-gatherers with poison arrows and loin cloths in pursuit of strange animals adapted to survive harsh conditions; of lions standing proud in the morning sun; of searing heat-hazed summers and icy winds howling over grassy plains. It is all of this and much more. It is one of the last places which remain larger than man's achievements, where the soul can soar untrammeled by signs of human development and where a journey can take on the dimensions of a pilgrimage."

Considering the mystery to me of how they find water for their survival, there was an amazing abundance of animals to be found in the desert. Water or moisture must be present some place, but certainly not found by humans such as ourselves. We had to carry 100 liters of water with us, not just for drinking or the radiator, but also for the coffee, cooking (potatoes, onions, and beans), cleaning the single cooking pot and two cups, brushing our teeth, but not for shaving. When I arrived back home I had acquired a beard, so I kept it as a reminder of life in the desert, which was a prayer.

During our time in the desert we slept in sleeping bags on the sand (would you believe how hot it can be during the day and yet how cold it can be at night?) and woke with the first light of day or the sound of animals. We celebrated the mass, with missal, host, and cup, there on the sand, with animals close around. The presence of the Lord was evident and experienced. In the morning, before the intense heat, we walked for a couple of hours, in separate directions, until the bright red 4x4 land cruiser (which we borrowed) was barely in view. And just BE. No word needed to be uttered, from the mind or the lips; the heart itself spoke, and the ears of the soul could hear the reply of God, "Do you believe that I am here and that I love you?"

In the very heart of the desert we came across a settlement of the Bushmen. At first we saw their huts which are simply made of grass in a beehive shape. Inside, as we saw later, their cover against the cold of the night was the skins of animals. They came old and young, running to the land cruiser in greeting and curiosity. There was no option but the art of communication — without language. Having spent much time with the children of our deaf school helped in speaking with the hands and using expressions. Their language was particularly colorful with the clicks with complimented their gestures and expressions.

The children were particularly delightful in their simple purity, innocence, and beauty of character. To pick up these little children, I felt I was holding a gem more precious than all the diamonds

of Botswana. To gaze into their eyes was like looking into a clear pure brook before it runs into polluted rivers and becomes part of the pollution;
before it has a chance to become tainted in any way.
To experience these children was a prayer in itself.

When allowing the sanctity of the moment to
be blurred by the thought of the vast corruption in
our modern world and <u>the deterioration perpetrated by the decadent values which are constantly before people's eyes in the Western media</u>, it gave me
cause to wonder who are the real privileged people
in our world; who are the most content and happy
with themselves and their society; who are most in
touch with and at peace with self and nature and
God. It made me wonder what it really means to
be civilized. Is our concept of development really
a step forward or is it regression in regard to the
authentic values of life and love. The brief meeting
with the simple Bushmen provided much food for

thought, more to reflect on and even more to pray about.

Would that we could be plucked out of the contaminated waters of the so-called progressive society and be returned to the brookwater purity and simplicity that once was, but has long since been polluted <u>by so much of what is being placed before our eyes.</u>

ENDNOTES

1   St. Michael and the Angels, Tan Books and Publishers, Inc., Rockford, IL, 1983, p. 84.
2   Webster's New Collegiate Dictionary, G. & C. Merriam Co.
3   Ibid.
4   "Paul Harvey News Program."
5   Air Waves From Hell, Father Frank Poncelet, The Newman Press, Long Prairie, MN, 1991, p. 84.
6   Confidential, private interview with Caritas of Birmingham.
7   A Model for Renewal, 30 Days, Robert Mayniham, Sept.–Oct. 1990, pp. 58–59.
8   Webster's New Collegiate Dictionary, G. & C. Merriam Co.
9   A Pictorial History of Television, Second Enlarged Edition, Irving Settel, Frederick Ungar Publishing Co., NY, 1983, p. 19.
10   Ibid., p. 15.
11   Ibid., p. 19.
12   Ibid., p. vii.
13   Ibid., p. viii.
14   "Paul Harvey News Program."
15   A Pictorial History of Television, Second Enlarged Edition, Irving Settel, Frederick Ungar Publishing Co., NY, 1983, p. vii.
16   Ibid., pp. xi–xii.
17   Relayed by Fr. Al Winshman in his interview with Caritas of Birmingham.
18   A Pictorial History of Television, Second Enlarged Edition, Irving Settel, Frederick Ungar Publishing Co., NY, 1983, p. ix.
19   Interview with Fr. Al Winshman by Caritas of Birmingham.
20   Half an Hour With the Servants of God, Murphy & McCarthy, NY, 1889, Chapter XCIII.
21   Ibid., Chapter XCIII.
22   Ibid., Chapter XCIII.
23   Ibid., Chapter XCIII.
24   Ibid., Chapter XCIII.
25   Air Waves From Hell, Father Frank Poncelet, The Newman Press, Long Prairie, MN, 1991, p. 93.
26   Ibid., p. 93.
27   Pope Pius XII Encyclical, Miranda Prorus, pg. 226–227
28   Associated Press, Monday, March 11, 1996.
29   Half an Hour With the Servants of God, Murphy & McCarthy, NY, 1889, Chapter XCIII.
30   Talk given by Fr. Jozo to group of pilgrims on August 18, 1996 at Siroki Brijeg.
31   Scientific and Medical Studies on the Apparitions at Medjugorje, Fr. Rene Laurentin and Dr. Henri Joyeaux, Veritas Publications, 1987, p. 91.
32   Introduction to the Devout Life, St. Francis De Sales, TAN Publishers, 1990, p. 259.

33 Interview with Fr. Al Winshman by Caritas of Birmingham.
34 The Bible on Sex, Fr. Albert Lauer, Presentation Ministries, Cincinnati, OH, 1987, p. 17.
35 Les Brown's Encyclopedia of Television, Third Ed., Les Brown, Visible Ink Press, Detroit, MI, 1992, p. 349.
36 Ibid., pp. xi.
37 A Pictorial History of Television, Second Enlarged Edition, Irving Settel, Frederick Ungar Publishing Co., NY, 1983, p. viii.
38 Ibid., pp. 148–149.
39 Ibid., pp. viii.
40 The Perfect Machine - Television and the Bomb, Joyce Nelson, New Society Publishers, Phila., PA, 1992, pp. 69–80.
41 A Pictorial History of Television, Second Enlarged Edition, Irving Settel, Frederick Ungar Publishing Co., NY, 1983, p. ix.
42 The Perfect Machine - Television and the Bomb, Joyce Nelson, New Society Publishers, Phila., PA, 1992, p 71.
43 Ibid., pp. 72–73.
44 Ibid., p. 72.
45 Ibid., p. 145.
46 Ibid., p. 95.
47 Ibid., p. 95.
48 Ibid., p. 80.
49 Ibid., p. 80.
50 Ibid., p. 146.
51 Ibid., p. 146.
52 Ibid., p. 151.
53 Ibid., p. 151.
54 The Age of Television, Martin Esslin, Copyright ©1982 by Martin Esslin. Used with permission of W. H. Freeman and Co., San Francisco, CA, p. 80.
55 Breaking the TV Habit, Joan Anderson Wilkins, reprinted with permission of Scribner, an imprint of Simon & Schuster, copyright ©1982 Joan Anderson Wilkins, p. 154.
56 Less TV, Less Crime?, Irving Kristol, published in Focus on the Family Citizen, Oct. 17, 1994, p. 24.
57 Air Waves From Hell, Father Frank Poncelet, The Newman Press, Long Prairie, MN, 1991, p. 51.
58 Taped interview with Fr. Benedict J. Groeschel by Caritas of Birmingham.
59 Air Waves From Hell, Father Frank Poncelet, The Newman Press, Long Prairie, MN, 1991, p. 55.
60 The Navarre Bible — Revelation —Text and Commentaries, James Gavigan, Brian McCarthy, Thomas McGovern, using the Revised Standard Version and New Vulgage with a commentary by members of the Faculty of Theology of the University of Navarre, 1993, pp. 26–27.
61 Ibid., pp. 26–27.
62 Ibid., p. 18.
63 Ibid., pp. 128–129.
64 Ibid., p. 104.
65 Ibid., p. 98.

66 A Pictorial History of Television, Second Enlarged Edition, Irving Settel, Frederick Ungar Publishing Co., NY, 1983, p. vii.
67 Ibid., p. 20.
68 Ibid., p. 47.
69 The Perfect Machine - Television and the Bomb, Joyce Nelson, New Society Publishers, Phila., PA, 1992, p. 80.
70 A story relayed by theologian Fr. Rene Laurentin, in France.
71 Breaking the TV Habit, Joan Anderson Wilkins, reprinted with permission of Scribner, an imprint of Simon & Schuster, copyright ©1982 Joan Anderson Wilkins, p. 152.
72 Ibid., p. 160.
73 The Perfect Machine - Television and the Bomb, Joyce Nelson, New Society Publishers, Phila., PA, 1992, p. 145.
74 Ibid., p. 146.
75 Air Waves From Hell, Father Frank Poncelet, The Newman Press, Long Prairie, MN, 1991, p. 205.
76 "Cell Phone Addiction is so Real There's Rehab for it," https://www.shapc.com/lifestyle/mind-and-body/cell-phone-addiction-is-so-real-there's-rehab-for-it.
77 The Way - The Essential Classic of Opus Dei's Founder, Josemaria Escriva, 2005, p 110, #630.
78 Ibid., p. 110, #631.
79 Ibid.
80 Ibid., p. 110, #634
81 Ibid., p. 110, #636
82 Ibid.
83 "Steve Jobs Was a Low-Tech Parent," by Nick Bilton, The New York Times, September 10, 2014
84 The Washington Post, August 25, 2017
85 Ibid.
86 "Kids and Digital Demantia," by Heidi Wachter, https://experiencelife.com/article/kids-digital-dementia/, October 2015,
87 "The Health Risks of Tech Addiction," by Mo Perry, https://experiencelife.com/article/the-health-risks-of-tech-addiction/, April 2018
88 "The Mere Presence of a Cell Phone Maybe Distracting Implications for Attention and Talk Performance," by Bill Thornton, Alyson Faires, Maija Robbin and Eric Rollins, University of Southern Maine, 2014
89 "Will Our Children be Victims of Digital Dementia?, by Trace Embry
90 "The Mere Presence of a Cell Phone Maybe Distracting Implications for Attention and Talk Performance," by Bill Thornton, Alyson Faires, Maija Robbin and Eric Rollins, University of Southern Maine, 2014.
91 "How to Break Free of Tech Addiction," Mo Perry, April 2018
92 Ibid.
93 "The Health Risks of Tech Addiction," by Mo Perry, https://experiencelife.com/article/the-health-risks-of-tech-addiction/, April 2018
94 Ibid.
95 "Reading Comprehension: Print vs. Screen," Experieince Life, April 2017
96 Ibid.
97 Ibid.

98   Ibid.
99   Ibid.
100 *"Will Our Children be Victims of Digital Dementia?*, by Trace Embry
101 Ibid.
102 *"Kids and Digital Dementia,"* by Heidi Wachter, https://experiencelife.com/article/kids-digital-dementia/, October 2015,
103 Ibid.
104 Ibid.
105 Ibid.
106 Ibid.
107 Ibid.
108 Ibid.
109 Ibid.
110 *Will Our Children be Victims of Digital Dementia?*, by Trace Embry
111 *"Just Say No to Children's Screen Time,"* by Michael Dregni, May 2019
112 Ibid.
113 Ibid.
114 Ibid.
115 Ibid.
116 Ibid.
117 Ibid.
118 Ibid.
119 Ibid.
120 Ibid.
121 Ibid.
122 Ibid.
123 Ibid.
124 Ibid.
125 Ibid.
126 Ibid.
127 Ibid.
128 Ibid.

The Book for Our Time

We are witnessing defining moments in our nation and the world. A Friend of Medjugorje is showing very clearly, the role that Our Lady is playing, in what many do not even see as the work of God taking place in our midst.

"…didn't sleep til I finished reading <u>Big Q Little Q</u>. Immediately shared it with friends…"

— Ron
Makati, Philippines

MP3 Audio Book

Softcover Books

Audio Book 3-CD Set

See the order form in the back of the book to order.

The Economic
Time Bomb
is Ticking...

Are You Ready?

A Friend of Medjugorje tells you how to be ready for what is coming down soon.

"My son-in-law says: *'people do know how bad things are, but they don't know what to do.'* This book tells you <u>what to do right now</u>…"

Jean
Viola, Arkansas

"Being of a different denomination, this book has opened my eyes to see a large conversion of souls in the very near future."

Brett
Birmingham, Alabama

In Uncertain Times
One Thing is Certain

Order Form

	I See Far—Expanded— Soft Cover Books BF104	*Please add shipping and handling* ☐ **1**=$7.00 ☐ **10**=$40.00 ($4.00 EA) (For case pricing see below.)	$
	Big Q Little Q: The Calm Before the Storm Soft Cover BF125	*(Please add shipping and handling)* ☐ **1**=$13.95 ☐ **10**=$69.50 ($6.95 EA) ☐ **5**=$49.75 ($9.95 EA) ☐ **20**=$79.00 ($3.95 EA) (For larger quantities call for discounted case pricing.)	$
	It Ain't Gonna Happen A Return to Truth Soft Cover Books BF108	*(Please add shipping and handling)* ☐ **1**=$15.00 ☐ **10**=$70 ($7.00 EA) (For larger quantities call for discounted case pricing.)	$
	The Corona Vision Soft Cover Books BF126	*(Please add shipping and handling)* ☐ **1**=$4.00 ☐ **10**=$30 ($3.00 EA) ☐ **25**=$50 ($2.00 EA) ☐ **50**=$75 ($1.50 EA) (For larger quantities call for discounted case pricing.)	$
		Subtotal	$

Shipping & Handling

Order Sub-total	U.S. Mail *(Standard)*	UPS *(Faster)*	
$0–$10.00	$5.00	$15.00	For overnight delivery, call for pricing.
$10.01–$20.00	$7.50	$17.50	***International (Surface):**
$20.01–$50.00	$10.00	$20.00	**Double above shipping Cost.**
$50.01–$100.00	$15.00	$25.00	**Call for faster International delivery.**
Over $100.00	15% of total	25% of total	$

I See Far CASES OF 32 BOOKS **For Affordable, Easy Convenience**	*(UPS Shipping is included)*	
BF104–CASE CASES OF 32 ($1.75 EA) $56 + $45 S&H = $101.00	Cases QTY. TOTAL ☐ 1 32 $101.00 ☐ 2 64 $202.00 ☐ OTHER _____ ($101.00 EA)	$

Case orders are shipped UPS for faster trackable delivery.
For overnight delivery, call for pricing: 205-672-2000.
Call for international shipping costs.

TOTAL: $

☏ Ph: (Outside USA add 001)
205-672-2000 ext. 315 USA 24 hrs.
📠 Fax: **205-672-9667 USA 24 hrs.**
✉ Mail: **Caritas of Birmingham**
100 Our Lady Queen of Peace Drive
Sterrett, AL 35147-9987 USA

Enclose in remittance envelope or call in your order and donation.
If you have any questions you may call 205-672-2000 and leave a message on ext. 315.
Or call during office hours 8:30 a.m.–5:00 p.m. Central Time
Monday–Friday and talk with a real person ☺

The Federal Tax Exempt I.D. # for Caritas of Birmingham is 63-0945243.

Ship to: Name(s) (please print) _____ Birthday: _____
Address _____
City _____ State _____ Zip Code _____
Phone # _____(if an international number, include all digits)
☐Payment Enclosed
Credit Card type (check one) ☐ VISA ☐ MasterCard ☐ Discover
Credit Card Number ☐☐☐☐ ☐☐☐☐ ☐☐☐☐ ☐☐☐☐ 3-Digit Code on Back: ☐☐☐
Expiration date: ☐☐-☐☐ e-mail: _____

Job 2917 7/20/2020